HUNTER:
QUEBEC

ART WIEDERHOLD

Order this book online at www.trafford.com
or email orders@trafford.com

Most Trafford titles are also available at major online book retailers.

Printed in the United States of America.

ISBN: 978-1-4907-4598-5 (sc)
ISBN: 978-1-4907-4597-8 (e)

Trafford rev. 09/04/2014

www.trafford.com

North America & international
toll-free: 1 888 232 4444 (USA & Canada)
fax: 812 355 4082

INTRODUCTION

Quebec (Kebec) Huron for the place where the rivers run together. Founded in 1604 by the French, it soon became the cornerstone for Nouvelle France. Since it controlled the vital waterway known as the St. Lawrence River, it became one of the most fought-over pieces of real estate in North American history. British forces besieged the city four times over the 150 years and finally captured it after defeating the French on the Plains of Abraham west of the city's walls in 1759. American forces assailed it twice. Once during the American Revolution and again during the War of 1812-14. Both expeditions ended in disastrous defeats for the attackers. After the last attack, the British refortified the ancient walls and constructed an impregnable fortress on a bluff overlooking the city which they dubbed The Citadel.

During the era known as the Dark Times, an army of marauding bandits and thugs marched on Quebec in search of plunder. The host approached the city from the west and south. Although they were well-armed and numbered more than 30,000, they realized that no matter how hard they tried, they would never be able to breech those massive walls. Discouraged, the marauders turned away from Quebec and the city was left in peace.

Now, in the year289 SA, the city was again under siege . . .

CHAPTER ONE:
A Winter's Chill

A light snow fell over the ancient walled city, adding yet another layer to what had covered the ground for weeks. It had been an unusually cold winter, even for Quebec. The type of winter that occurs once in a man's lifetime-if at all.

Winter had arrived early. The first snow fell in mid-October, rushing ahead of the Arctic air mass that froze the waters of the St. Lawrence River solid. By early November, the river became impassable and the ice was so thick, even the two icebreakers couldn't get through it.

Nothing could get through that ice.

And the heavy snows made overland travel impossible.

Quebec was isolated.

The winter wasn't the city's only problem. The bitter cold had brought something else with it. Something unknown.

Terrifying.

Unspeakable.

Dr. Marcel LeVant stood at the gates of the cemetery and watched as three black hearses moved slowly past him. Each hearse was drawn by a team of black horses. Each had a black-draped casket in the back and two drivers, also dressed in black with top hats. They clattered over the cobblestoned road and slowly disappeared behind a row of ancient vaults.

"Three more for the Reaper," he sighed as dozens of mourners in black carriages moved past him and followed the hearses.

"That makes seven this past week," he thought. "More than three hundred since October."

LeVant was the chief medical officer for Quebec. He was 67 years old, medium height and built and had brown hair streaked with strands of silver. He wore pince nez glasses and sported a goatee. In his 45 years of practice, he had seen and successfully treated all sorts of ailments and injuries.

But never had he encountered anything like this.

The disease, if one could call it that, came out of nowhere. It struck young and old with a fierce indifference and brought even the strongest to their knees. It resembled influenza, but with a difference.

Everyone who came down with it ended up in the graveyard.

It had no initial warning symptoms. There was no fever. No rashes. No cough. Nothing at all to indicate one had become infected. Over four days, the victims became noticeably lethargic. By the fifth day, they were too weak to even get out of bed. That's when their tongues swelled to twice the normal size and they began twitching and screaming uncontrollably. By the sixth morning, they were dead.

He'd performed several autopsies. In each case, he was mystified to see that their hearts had burst and flooded their bodies with blood.

LeVant had tried everything he could think of. He'd even resorted to more ancient remedies and even prayer. But with each passing week, the body count mounted. He had no idea if it had spread to the outer villages as there had been no way to communicate with them. He wondered if the disease was confined to Quebec or more widespread.

He wondered how intense their suffering had been.

"What did they feel or think in their final moments?" he asked.

He was about to leave the cemetery when he heard footsteps behind him, He turned and scowled as Louis Giffe, the grave digger, ran up to him.

"We have another one, Doctor," Giffe said. "It's happened again."

"Show me," LeVant instructed.

Giffe led him up a side path to where another victim of the disease had been buried less than three days earlier. When LeVant saw the condition of the grave and the corpse lying within the open casket, he made the sign of the cross.

"Merciful God!" he said.

Twenty minutes later, he barged into the office of Governor-General Denis Marquand, a robustly built man with snow white hair and a handlebar mustache. He looked for the entire world like a British field commander of the 19th century. Before rising to his current office, he'd served as the commander of the Home Guard at the ancient fortress known as the Citadel, which overlooked the port and the city below.

As a soldier, he'd spent 30 years of his life living at the Citadel. As Governor-General, he still resided there.

With him at that time was Col. Yves Montcalm, the present commander of the Guard, who had a reputation for being a no nonsense, spit and polish officer. Montcalm was just 34 years old, lean and fit.

They listened as LeVant explained the goings on at the cemetery.

"Since November, we have buried over 300 victims of this plague. All but 6 have been dug up and desecrated," LeVant said. "The way things are going, I fully expect those who were buried this morning to suffer the same fate."

"What will you have me do, Doctor?" Marquand asked.

"I don't know, Denis. This has me at my wits end. There must be some way we can find out who or what is doing these terrible things. Maybe then, we can figure out how to make it stop," LeVant replied.

Marquand looked at Montcalm.

"I thought I ordered you to post a watchman at the cemetery," he said.

"I did, Monsieur. The last man I posted disappeared. We found nothing but his hat and rifle," Montcalm said.

"That makes three in the past week—along with all of the other disappearances," Marquand said.

"Disappearances?" LeVant asked. "You mean there are more?"

Marquand nodded.

"Since this winter began, 114 of our citizens have gone missing. All without a trace. I have an ugly feeling that the plague, the disappearances and the desecrations are somehow linked together. Usually, things are very peaceful in Quebec. This winter has brought us a nightmare with the snow," he said.

LeVant shook his head.

"I hope you are wrong, Denis," he said.

"Colonel—I want you to post a two-man guard on the cemetery. I want it guarded around the clock and rotate your men every two hours. If anything is going to happen, it will be within the next 72 hours. Maybe we'll get lucky this time," Marquand ordered.

He saw the look of dismay on LeVant's face.

"I am sorry, mon ami. That is the best I can. Our regiment is stretched very thin," he said.

"I understand, Denis. Merci," LeVant said as he left the office.

Montcalm rubbed his temples and looked at Marquand.

"I will do as you ask, Monsieur, but I think this will be as fruitless as before," he said.

"Single guards vanished. Two men can watch each others' backs and have a better chance of seeing something. I want to know what's doing this and if they have connections to those things that howl in the woods at night," Marquand said.

The disappearances always occurred during a howling session. Whenever anyone heard it, they knew someone else was about to turn up missing. Quebecois never feared the darkness until now. In fact, most people were terrified of it.

"And if we find out? Then what?" Montcalm asked.

"We try to kill or capture whatever it is so Doctor LeVant can study it. We need to know exactly what we are faced with, Colonel. We need to put a face to those things in the shadows," Marquand said.

"Are you sure you want to do that, Monsieur?" Montcalm asked. "We may not be prepared for such a thing."

"It is better to face fear than to live with it. Do as I've asked, Colonel. I want your best men assigned to this detail at all times. We must get to the bottom of this, regardless of the consequences," Marquand said.

Montcalm rose, saluted and left to carry out his orders.

There were only 1,000 men in the Home Guard. Three hundred were permanently based at the Citadel while the others were scattered throughout Quebec Province in smaller garrisons. The next largest contingent of 250 men, were housed at ancient Fort Stewart in Montreal. It was barely enough to cover the province.

He smiled.

There were times he thought he had too many soldiers. Now, he wondered if he had enough.

The city was protected by nearly five miles of high, stone ramparts. It had four well-protected heavy gates and over 200 artillery pieces. It had taken years to restore the guns to the point where they could fire again and all of his men were trained in their use. The main ramparts overlooked a wide, flat area that stretched to a cliff to the west. This was called the Plains of Abraham, after a French farmer who owned the land during the 1600s.

On a cliff overlooking the river at the southwestern end of the city stood the impregnable fortress called the Citadel. It was built during the early 1800s by the British and for nearly 200 years it was the home base for the crack Royal 22nd Regiment. During the wars that led up to the event known as the Great Disaster, the Royal 22nd was sent off to fight in Europe. When they left, they took all of their modern weapons and vehicles with them. The Regiment never returned to Quebec.

The then Governor-General, Jean Claude DeMenil, decided that Quebec needed troops to defend it. He gathered up several officers and sergeants of the 22nd who had retired in Quebec and tasked them with forming a Home Guard, at least 1,000 strong.

The 22nd had left behind some older 20th century and earlier period rifles and handguns. Ammunition and gunpowder, especially for the old muskets, was easy enough to manufacture and the new troops were trained and housed at the Citadel.

DeMenil decided that the uniforms should mirror those of the original French colonial troops who had defended Quebec during the 1700s. At least while they were garrisoned. Out in the field or on patrol outside the city walls, they wore the camouflaged uniforms of the 22nd.

After everyone was recruited and clad in the proper uniforms, they underwent years of rigorous training and drills which made them among the toughest, most skilled and best disciplined soldiers on Earth.

Over 1,200 years later, they still protected Quebec.

Except that now, they and a handful of red-uniformed Mounted Police, were responsible for the protection of the entire region known as Quebec. That meant two major cities, dozens of ancient villages and hamlets on both sides of the river and parts of the Huron Nation.

Montcalm sighed as he entered his office. Master Sergeant Francois Duchesne followed him and listened as he gave the orders. Duchesne was a well-seasoned soldier with more than 35 years of service in the Guard. When Montcalm was finished, Duchesne simply saluted and left as he always did.

Montcalm smiled.

All of the men in the Guard were like that. They carried out their orders without complaint. If they had opinions, they never voiced them to their officers. Every man knew exactly what was at stake. The Guard was the first and last line of defense for the people of Quebec. Although they had not been involved in any actual combat for the past generation, each man was trained to hold his ground against anything and everything that came at him. They would not retreat unless ordered to do so.

But they had been trained for combat against human foes. Montcalm wondered what strange and perhaps terrifying creatures now plagued Quebec and if his men would be able to stand their ground against them?

He looked through his office window at the darkening sky.

"What is out there?" he wondered.

At the Basilique-Cathedrale Notre-Dame, the city's chief religious advisor, Fr. Bruno Challons, had just finished an early morning baptism of a baby boy. His aide presented the happy parents with the baptism shawl and a new rosary. Then Fr. Challons presented them with a small bottle of holy water from the baptismal basin and thanked them for their faith. He watched as he aide escorted them out, then returned to his office.

LeVant was seated next to his desk sipping coffee. Challons smiled, poured himself a large cup of the black brew and sat down.

"And yet another child is initiated into our flock," he smiled. "He appears to be a fine, healthy child, too."

LeVant nodded. Challons had baptized his children over the years. Challons father had baptized LeVant. Things in Quebec tended to span generations. Since everything had worked so very well for centuries, no one saw the need to change.

"Did you send that letter, Bruno?" LeVant asked.

"Of course. I mailed it several weeks ago—before the river froze over completely. It should have arrived in Rome in December. Now, it's up to the Cardinal. He must decide if our situation calls for more professional assistance," Challons replied.

"I didn't know the Vatican existed until you informed me," LeVant said. "I always believed the Slayers to be an old wives' tale."

"The Slayers have been plying their skills for centuries, mon ami. They work in the shadows, like those things out there. Although they prefer to remain anonymous, some have become quite famous over the years. We are undergoing something strange and dark that we can't even begin to understand. That's why I suggested it," Challons said.

"Do you think they'll send help?" LeVant asked.

"The Cardinal is an old friend of mine. I'm sure he will send his best people to investigate," Challons assured him. "Be patient, Marcel. Such things take time. This is not like the First Age when our ancestors could simply pick up a telephone and call for help. We must rely on the mail, like in the very old days."

"I hope we *have* time, Bruno," LeVant said.

"Put your trust in God and believe," Challons advised.

"Which god? Ours or the god of those things out there?" LeVant asked sarcastically. "I have little faith in gods these days."

"I understand," Challons said. "Whether you believe or not, there is little for us to do right now but wait. And watch the shadows."

LeVant laughed.

"I used to enjoy the night hours before this began. Now, I fear them like everyone else in Quebec," he said.

"Our ancestors feared the night. Perhaps they were plagued by these very same things?' Challons suggested. "We Quebecois like to tell ourselves that we avoided the Dark Times after the rest of civilization collapsed. But did we?"

LeVant shrugged.

"Recent events makes one wonder, does it not?" he asked.

"Indeed," Challons said.

Portneuf.

Forty five miles to the southwest of Quebec stood Redoubt Portneuf. Most of the year, it was manned by two full companies of the Guard. When winter set in, the number was reduced by half and the rest were withdrawn to the Citadel to await the spring thaw. The Redoubt was self sufficient. The men grew and canned their own vegetables and hunted deer, moose and elk and fished in local lakes and rivers. They also kept the sheds supplied with enough firewood to keep their barracks warm and stoves going through the winter months. The unit also had its own doctor who ran the post's clinic.

The commander, Capt. Luc Roche, had been with the Guard for 18 years. He had been assigned to his post back in July. Since Portneuf was considered a very quiet post, it was the ideal place to start out new officers.

The redoubt was made of granite and brick like the Citadel. It contained a three story barracks, a long, one story mess hall, an armory, officers quarters, a command center and stables. The buildings were clustered around a wide, rectangular parade and training field and the entire redoubt was surrounded by 20 foot high stone ramparts. There was one large gate in the wall facing east. A gravel road led from the redoubt to nearby Portneuf, a village of about 2,000 people. Both overlooked a bend in the river.

When Roche took command of the Redoubt, he never imagined it would be anything like this.

Just days after half his men were withdrawn, the river froze over and blizzards closed down every road into and out of Portneuf. He kept his men busy clearing snow from the redoubt and trying to keep the road to the village open. That wasn't so bad. Such things are expected during winter in Quebec.

About a week later, things began to happen.

Strange things.

A handful of the villagers came down with a mysterious ailment that not even the regimental doctor could identify or treat. Within days, all of the villagers were dead. Roche was at the cemetery when they were buried and after they were interred, he thought that was the end of it.

That's when things got really weird.

Within three days after the burials, the villagers discovered that all of the graves had been dug up and the coffins had been broken into. To his horror, he discovered that something had partially eaten the corpses.

Some sort of animals driven to desperation by the deep snow?

He decided to send his best trackers out to find them. After four days, they returned empty-handed. Three more villagers died a week later. They, too, were buried in the old cemetery. Three days later, the villagers discovered that their graves had also been desecrated. The mayor asked Roche to have his men guard the cemetery after the next round of funerals. He agreed and posted two of his best men near the fresh graves.

Three days later, not only had the graves been violated but his men had gone missing. All they could find were their fur hats, a strap with a canteen attached, and their rifles. Neither had been fired and there were no signs of a struggle.

That was the night they first heard the high-pitched howls.

Then villagers started to go missing in the night.

First one a week.

Then two or three.

They vanished without a trace. The villagers became terrified of the dark and now barricaded themselves into their homes as soon as the sun set. But even that didn't p[protect them from the strange plague.

They still died.

They were still buried in the old cemetery.

And their graves were still being desecrated.

And each night, the howling grew louder.

And closer.

The sound of footsteps approaching snapped Roche out of his reverie. He turned and smiled as Lt. Perry Brande, the regimental doctor came up and saluted. Roche returned it.

"Report, Doctor," he said.

"I have just completed my examination of Private LeRoi, Sir," the doctor said. "It is just as I feared. He has all of the same symptoms as the people in the village. I've placed him in the isolation ward as a precaution."

"Are you certain it's the plague?" Roche asked.

"Oui, mon Capitan. There is no doubt," the doctor replied.

"I see. Do what you can for him," Roche said in resignation. "And try to keep it from spreading to the rest of the company."

The doctor turned smartly and hurried back to the clinic. Roche watched and sighed.

"It was only a matter of time," he said as he continued to his office.

Directly across the river from Quebec was the small port of Levis. Levis was nearly as ancient as the walled city itself and it hugged the waterfront at the base of some high mountains. It was a fishing village during the warm months. This winter, it had nearly frozen over.

Levis was the biggest town close to Quebec. It boasted over two miles of fishing docks, more than two dozen inns and hotels, large shops and open air markets, saloons, clubs and several old churches. At the height of its glory during the First Age, it had over 138,000 residents. But the Dark Years before the Second Age had produced a plague that had nearly wiped out the entire population. Those who could, moved to Quebec and Montreal to avoid it and Levis became a ghost town for a while.

Over the last 150 years, it had undergone a renaissance and the population steadily increased as more families moved into and restored many of the fine old homes and buildings. Now, Levis have over 25,000 residents and it was still growing.

Standing on the heights above the city were the crumbling remains of old Fort Number One, which was constructed by the British along with two other small forts in 1872. The other forts were gone by the end of the 20th century of the First Age. Number One was restored and used as a park and museum for the next 200 years. It was abandoned altogether along with Levis.

Now, two dozen rusted artillery pieces still stood upon the crumbling masonry ramparts overlooking the St. Lawrence River.

Levis could easily be seen from the Terrasse Dufferin and was normally reached by ferry. Now, virtually buried beneath several feet of snow, the only things still visible were its bright red roofs and church spires.

Montcalm stood on the battlements of the Citadel and looked out toward Levis. He could see wisps of smoke rising out of the chimneys of several buildings, but they were the only signs of life over there. The fleet of fishing boats was trapped in the harbor by sheets of ice. Even the ferry had been frozen into its dock.

No one could get into or out of Levis until the spring thaw.

But the lack of lights after sunset disturbed Montcalm. Normally, the taverns and restaurants stayed open late each night as people gathered in those places for a good meal, strong drinks and entertainment. The freezing cold had never stopped the people of Levis from enjoying life to its fullest.

But lately, the windows of the buildings remained dark and Levis was quiet at night.

Too damned quiet.

"Just what is happening over there?" Montcalm wondered.

The frozen river had also cut off all contact with the ancient villages on Ile-D'Orleans just to the east. There were five small villages over there and a platoon of the Home Guard stationed at a redoubt in St. Francois on the northeastern tip of the Ile. Even the ancient bridge had frozen over. That made travel by horse or wagons impossible as well.

Had the people of Levis also been visited by the same strange events that plagued Quebec? Or were they somehow immune?

Levis.

Leonard Haynes was in his late 50s, broad shouldered, strong and had collar length thick, black hair, a bushy beard and a handlebar mustache. He was a part-time fisherman and the full-time mayor of Levis and had been for the past 22 years. Before that, he served 12 years in the Home Guard. He had a reputation for being brutally honest and was afraid of nothing.

Except spiders.

For some reason, the arachnids scared the daylight out of him.

His friends joked with him about it and even placed spiders where he'd see them just to watch his reaction. Haynes took their pranks good-naturedly and even laughed at himself for being scared of such tiny creatures.

Levis lay under several feet of snow. In some places, the snow was so deep one could only see the bright red roofs of single story homes sticking out of it. He and his friends had spent parts of many days and nights shoveling people out of their houses and making sure they were alright.

Everyone was.

Deep snows were normal for this time of year. Most people had prepared for the winter by stocking up on canned items and necessities, such as firewood and lamp oil. No one froze to death in Levis.

In fact, this winter, no one had even gotten sick or died. It had been a remarkably healthy winter. Haynes stopped shoveling his walk to chat with his neighbors. The ice was thicker this year, they said. Thicker than normal.

Thicker than anyone could remember it ever being.

But no one seemed frustrated or angry about it. The people of Levis simply took it in stride. They were a tough lot. They worked hard. They drank hard. They lived their lives to the fullest and rarely felt down.

They even partied at funerals.

But not this winter.

Haynes looked across at the lights of Quebec. There'd been no contact with the city since the river iced over. But the lights gleamed brightly and all seemed as usual.

He had no idea what was happening over there.

If he knew, it would scare him much more than the spiders.

St. Francois, Ile D'Orleans.

Captain Robert Pike watched as the unit physician, Herbert Norris, administered yet another dose of antibiotics to each of the men in the small dispensary. There were three in all. Each had come down with mysterious symptoms only two days ago. Whatever it was had forced Norris to confine all three to beds.

As Norris gave the third man his injection, he smiled weakly and put the syringes back into his bag. Then he pulled the blankets up so they covered the soldier from chin to toes and walked out with Pike.

"What is it?" Pike asked.

"I'm not sure, Robert," Norris replied. "At first, I thought it was influenza. But this is too fast acting. The men are very weak and listless. Whatever it is, it's draining the life from them."

"Is it contagious?" Pike asked as they walked back to his office.

Norris shrugged.

"So far, no one else has come down with it," he said. "But it's too early to tell."

"What about the people in the village? Have any of them come down with this?" Pike asked as they entered the building.

"I have heard there were two such cases last week," Norris said as he sat down in the tall backed leather chair next to Pike's desk.

Pike poured them each a cup of hot coffee and sat down. He passed Norris one of the cups.

"How are they?" he asked.

"Both died four days after contracting this," Norris replied as he sipped the hot beverage. "They buried them both yesterday. But those are the only cases I've heard of—so far."

"Dead? You mean this illness is fatal?" Pike asked.

"For them it was," Norris answered with a smirk.

"What about our men? Will they die, too?" asked Pike.

"Not if I can help it, Robert," Norris said. "I will do everything in my power to make sure they will recover. You know I will."

Pike nodded.

He had 47 soldiers fit for duty. Right now, the heavy snows had trapped them inside the tiny redoubt. The roads to the nearest town were impassable, thanks to a blizzard the night before. No one could reach the village and no one in the village of 1,800 people could get out. They were also cut off from the other villages on the island.

If this was the start of an epidemic, they would be effectively quarantined from the rest of Quebec. And in such close quarters as the redoubt, the effects would be devastating to say the least.

He smiled at Norris.

"Do whatever you can for them, Herb," he said. "And watch the other men for any signs of infection."

"Will do," Norris agreed. "I wish I knew what this was. Once I identify it, I may be able to affect a cure. Right now, I'm flying blind."

Lauren Lamour was the mayor of St. Francois. She was 38, tall, blonde and trim. Her late husband, Jules, had been the city treasurer. A year earlier, he attempted to abscond with half the city's finances and Lauren's cousin, Babette. When Lauren found about it, she loaded Jules' pistol and hunted them down. She found them walking together in the town square and opened fire.

She shot Jules twice in the chest. She shot Babette once in her left knee and a second time in her right ankle. Then she stormed off cursing at the top of her lungs much to amusement of the locals who had witnessed her tantrum.

Jules died of his wounds two days later.

Babette limped out of town on crutches a week after.

Lauren had Jules cremated. She took his ashes home and poured them into the toilet. After adding her own bodily fluids to them, she flushed. Jules had always wanted a burial at sea and this was the most fitting, given the circumstances.

She then packed up all of his belongings and gave them to the church charity. She burned all of his photos and flushed those ashes down the same toilet.

Instead of having her arrested for murder, the grateful townspeople elected her mayor. Partly for ridding them of her scumbag husband. Mostly for saving their funds.

Besides, they realized that Lauren was not to be trifled with.

She quickly started a hot and heavy affair with her personal assistant, a younger man named Carl Bergere. She was also having an affair with her dear friend, Dr. Gens Deaver, who was also the head of the city's health department. She had a lot of lost time to make up for and she threw herself into her work with incredible gusto.

On this cold, cloudy Tuesday afternoon, Dr. Deaver became the bearer of strange tidings. He dropped in to see her in her office at the city hall and relayed the bizarre news.

"Are you sure, Gens?" she asked incredulously.

"Quite sure, Lauren," Deaver replied. "I examined the sites myself this morning. Both graves had been dug up and the coffins broken into. When I examined the bodies, I realized that each had been partially eaten. There was no mistaking it!"

Bergere winced.

"What eats corpses?" he asked.

"Starving animals, perhaps?" Lauren suggested.

"I thought of that. But animals leave tracks in the snow. Any animals that dug up those graves would have left hundreds of tracks. Yet I found none. There were none going to or away from the graves. Nothing at all," Deaver said.

She stared at him.

"Those people were buried only three days ago. The bodies were still fresh," Deaver added.

"Then whatever did this needed to feed on fresh corpses?" Bergere asked.

Deaver shrugged.

"All I can say with any certainty is that the bodies were partially eaten. What did it remains a mystery," he said.

The mayor walked to her window and looked out at the workers who were attempting to clear paths through the snow that blanketed the ground. It was just so the locals could get around easier. The main roads were still buried. In effect, St. Francois was shut down.

"We have to inform Captain Pike of this," she decided. "Get over to the redoubt, Carl. I don't care how, but do it. Pike has to know of this."

Bergere nodded.

"I'll get there even if I have to shovel a path all the way to the redoubt," he said. "Do you think this is a military matter?"

"Perhaps not. But this is a police matter and Pike's soldiers are also the police," she said. "Just get it done, Carl."

Bergere nodded again and left the office. She sat down behind her desk and looked Deaver in the eyes.

"So, what kind of creature does eat dead bodies?" she asked.

"I haven't the faintest clue, Lauren. But I get the feeling that we will soon find out. When that happens, we are sure not to like it," he said.

Montreal.

One hundred fifty miles to the west, in the ancient city of Montreal, Mayor Tomas Bourgue looked out through his office window at the falling snow. Bourgue was tall, dark haired and athletic. He had been elected mayor only one month earlier after his predecessor died of the mysterious plague. His was the 175th such death since winter began.

But that wasn't the worst of it.

Each time they buried someone in the cemeteries that lay just outside the city's walls, their graves had been desecrated within 72 hours and parts of the corpses had been eaten. Then there were the disappearances. At least 30 people had gone missing within the last three months. Most vanished during the night while out shopping or on their way home from work. The disappearances had caused the people of Montreal to fear the darkness. Instead of frequenting the clubs, taverns and theaters as they had for centuries, most people simply stayed at home after sunset. Nightlife in the city had ground to a virtual halt.

He couldn't blame them, either.

Who could enjoy an evening on the town when you had to constantly look over your shoulder or watch the shadows?

Montreal was nearly as ancient as Quebec. It was established in 1611 of the First Age by the same explorer who founded Quebec. At first, it was a series of small forts and trading posts along the St. Lawrence River. Later, stone walls connected the forts and protected the port and the settlement at Mont Royal. The walls served the city well through several sieges but when Canada fell to the British in 1760, things changed.

The original fortifications were razed between 1800-1817 and Montreal quickly expanded beyond the Old City and port and the population swelled to more than three million. Like most ancient cities that survived the Great Disaster and the Dark Times that followed, Montreal experienced an almost brutal decline. Disease and invasions by barbaric armies had forced the people to abandon most of the outer parts of the city and concentrate in the older neighborhoods along the river and Old Port. By then, the city managers had reconstructed the ancient battlements to protect themselves from invaders and established a branch of the Home Guard to keep the city safe.

The walls followed the old city plans almost exactly. They stood 20 feet high and were 20 feet thick. There were eight turreted gates and a dozen barracks. Artillery pieces overlooked the river and Old Port and the areas to the west, north and east of the walls. The Mont Royal area was also fortified and both places were linked by an underground system of tunnels and streets that had existed since the 20th century of the First Age.

In the middle of the river were the tiny islands of Ste. Helene and Notre Dame. In the center of Ste. Helene was ancient Fort Stewart. This brick and mortar citadel was constructed by the British in the late 1700s and had fallen into disuse during the Dark Times. Twenty years earlier, the city managers and the commander of the Home Guard decided to restore the fort, which was now the permanent home for two companies of the Guard along with 24 artillery pieces. Anyone who was bold enough to try to attack Montreal by river would have to sail past not only the guns of Fort Stewart but also the 36 guns along the ramparts of the Rue de la Commune.

But it wasn't attack from human foes Bourgue feared. What currently plagued the old city was something no one could understand or see. Something that the walls and guns could not keep out.

Something that had arrived on the heels of the unusually bitter winter and dwelled in the deep shadows.

"How does one defend against that?" he wondered.

A knock on the door interrupted his thoughts. He turned and faced the door.

"Entres vous!" he called.

A short, stocky man dressed in the red jacket and blue striped pants of the Mounted Police entered. He was Victor Gaude, the commander of the Montreal Police Force.

"We've just received another missing persons report, Tomas," he said. "It's a woman named Isabelle LeMay. She never made it home from work last night, so her husband reported her missing."

"I see. How many does that make now?" Bourgue asked.

"Thirty four," Gaude replied.

"Send out the usual search parties, although I doubt it will be of any use," Bourgue ordered.

"They are already out there, Tomas. They've been out searching for the past six hours without any luck. It's just like the others," Gaude said. "Who do you suppose is taking them?"

"To be honest, Victor, I am almost afraid to find out," Bourgue answered. "Has there been any word from the redoubt?"

"Nothing since before the blizzard. Since the river is frozen and the roads are buried under several feet of snow, we can't reach them and they can't reach us. We haven't heard from anyone anywhere, Tomas. It's like we are the only remaining city on Earth," Gaude said. "We are completely isolated."

"And up to our necks in trouble," Bourgue added.

Fort Stewart.

Lt. Guy Passant was seated before the fireplace sipping hot maple tea from a large mug when he heard a knock at his door.

"Entres!" he called.

He sneezed just as Sgt. Randalf LaMont came in from the blizzard.

"Damn this snow! I'm sick of it already!" LaMont said as he stamped it from his boots.

Passant looked at him.

This was their fifth year at Fort Stewart. LaMont usually left with half the company each winter. This year, he decided to remain. It was a decision he'd regretted since early November.

"I always believed these heavy overcoats of ours could keep out even the bitterest cold. I guess I was wrong," he said as he poured himself a mug of tea and sat down. "How is your cold, Guy?" he asked as he sipped.

"A little better, merci," Passant replied. "At least my fever has broken. How are the men?"

"As usual. I know they don't like this bitter cold any more than we do, yet I have not heard a single complaint from any of them. They are toughing it out like the soldiers they are," LaMont said as he looked at the flames crackling over the logs.

"Two more of the locals have gone missing. That makes seven so far this month," he said.

"And 19 since winter set in," Passant counted. "And all vanished without leaving behind even the slightest of clues."

"By the way, the local butcher, Jonathan Ford, died this morning. He was only 51 years old, too," LaMont said.

"How did he die?" Passant queried as he fought off a sudden urge to shiver.

"His wife told me that he had taken ill last week. He seemed to be doing well. Then, when she tried to wake him this morning, he didn't move. He was barely breathing so she hurried to get the doctor. By the time he arrived, Msr. Ford had expired," LaMont said.

"You make him sound like a carton of milk," Passant smiled. "Did you speak with Doctor Abraham?"

"Oui. He said that Msr. Ford had caught some sort of virus. Sort of like influenza. He seemed to be recovering until this morning," LaMont replied.

He smiled at Passant.

"You'd best take good care of yourself, mon ami. I do not wish to inherit command of this fort by default," he said.

Passant laughed.

Then coughed.

LaMont waited for the spasm to pass and sipped his tea. Passant stopped, cleared his throat, and smiled.

"I'll be alright," he assured him. "The worst has passed."

"That's what poor Jonathan thought, too," LaMont said with a smile. "Then, before he knew it, poof! And he was gone."

"Has anyone else caught that virus?" Passant asked.

"Not that I am aware of. As far as I know, Ford was the first. Hopefully, he will be the last," LaMont answered.

"Just to be certain, ask Dr. Abraham to stop by the fort this evening and examine each of the men," Passant said.

LaMont nodded.

"Good idea, Guy. It's best to play such things safe, eh," he said.

He finished his tea. Passant watched as he stood and put the heavy overcoat back on. He buttoned it up and donned his fur hat.

"I'll see you at the noon mess, eh?" he said.

"I will be there," Passant promised.

LaMont opened the door and stepped back into the blizzard. Just as he pulled the door shut behind him, Passant heard him curse at the snow.

CHAPTER TWO:
On a Midnight Clear

New Orleans, two weeks later

Hunter drew his revolver as he entered the crumbling old church. The ancient edifice had stood abandoned for countless decades and made an ideal hiding place for a vampire. It sat on the edge of the bayou just 15 miles north of Lake Ponchartrain and once been the predominant structure in the small community that had long ago been reclaimed by the swamp.

The vampire and his brides, had taken up residence in the church which was within easy striking distance of New Orleans. Over a period of three weeks, they had claimed six victims. Two had been turned and were now his brides. They had been very good at covering their tracks. And the vampires thought that no one would imagine they'd be hiding in an abandoned church.

No one but Hunter, that is.

As he walked along the rubble strewn aisle, Hunter sensed that several pairs of eyes were watching him. He smiled and looked around.

"Come out, come out, whoever you are!" he challenged.

No answer.

He continued to walk toward the altar and watched the shadows. He stopped at the rail and looked around.

"Doesn't anyone here want to come out and play with me?" he called. "Anyone at all?"

The vampire watched Hunter from the choir loft. From his garb, he knew he was a Slayer. From the strong steady heartbeat, he knew this one was virtually fearless. He hadn't come to New Orleans to do battle against a Slayer. Had he known one was here, he would have set up house somewhere else. He didn't find out about the Slayer until Hunter stepped into the church.

Hunter suddenly turned, looked up into the choir and fired his revolver. The shot narrowly missed the startled vampire and shattered one of the rusted organ pipes behind him.

"How on Earth did he see me?" he wondered as he dodged a second shot. This one tore a path through his jacket sleeve.

Hunter heard a door creak to his left and turned just as two female vampires charged at him. He seized the first one by the throat, lifted her in the air, whirled around and slammed her to the floor. The impact broke the ancient floorboards and she ended up in the cellar. The second leaped onto his back. He reached back, grabbed her by the hair and hurtled her across the room. She struck the altar with enough force to shatter it and ended up buried beneath a mountain of wood, plaster and bronze trimmings. The first vampire leapt out of the hole in the floor only to get shot in the face. The impact sent her spinning back into the hole and she cursed him as she fell. Hunter walked to the altar and waited as the second vampire clawed her way out of the debris. He drew his katana and decapitated her just as she brushed the last bit of dust from her dress. As soon as her body hit the floor, he took a wooden stake from his mantle and rammed it through her chest. Her heart burst like a water-filled balloon and she lay still after a few ugly spasms.

The vampire in the choir was stunned.

"Who are you?" he asked.

"Hunter!" came the reply.

All of the color drained from the vampire's face when he heard the name. He realized he was in way over his head and nothing good would come from this confrontation. He decided to flee through the side door.

That's when a beautiful, red-haired woman stepped into view and blocked the exit.

"Going somewhere?" she asked as she delivered a slap across his face that sent him staggering back into the organ.

He hit it and landed on his knees. He rubbed his face as she stood back up and glared at her. The blow had actually stung.

"No human woman could deliver such a blow," he said.

"You're right," she said as she bared her fangs.

He laughed and attacked, determined to fight his way past her and escape into the swamp. She grabbed his right wrist and gave it sudden, violent, sharp twist. He felt his bone snap like a dry twig and grimaced at the pain. He lashed out with his other hand, but she ducked under it and grabbed him by the throat. Before he could react, she sank her fangs into his neck.

As soon as they penetrated his vein, he became immobilized. All he could do now was stand there while she drained the life from him. Two minutes later, she tossed his dead and bloodless corpse out of the choir. He landed in the center of the aisle with a loud crash. Hunter walked up and decapitated him. He then dragged his body over to where the one of the females lay.

Lorena came down, picked up the vampire's head and threw it on the pile.

There was no need for Hunter to drive a stake through his heart. When one vampire slays another, that vampire stays dead. But they always burned their bodies as a precaution.

Hunter took a bottle of blessed oil from his pocket, opened it and sprinkled it over the bodies. He struck a match and ignited the oil. Then he and Lorena left the church just as the flames began to spread.

"What about the other vampire?" asked Lorena as they mounted their horses. "She still lives."

"She doesn't seem to have the will for another fight and I don't feel like going into the cellar after her. If she has any sense, she'll leave New Orleans," he replied as they watched the flames consume the old church.

"And if she doesn't leave?" Lorena asked.

"You already know the answer to that, my love," he said as they rode away.

Two hours later, a dirty and half-terrified young vampire rose from the ashes of the church and brushed the debris from her tattered dress. She looked around to make sure Hunter and his wife were gone, them made her way north into the swamp.

She didn't know where she was going. She just wanted to get as far away from those Slayers as she could and as fast as she could. Even though New Orleans was her home, she knew she could never go back.

Not while Hunter lived there.

Hunter and Lorena reached New Orleans just as the sun burned its way through the early morning mist. It was a cool December day in the city. Cooler than usual for this time of year. They rode back to their house in the Garden District. As they dismounted, Hunter spotted the all-too-familiar envelope lying on the porch. He picked it up and opened it.

"It's from the Cardinal," he said as he read the letter. "He needs us to go to Quebec as soon as the spring thaw arrives. They're having all sorts of trouble up there."

"What sort of trouble?" asked Lorena.

"He didn't say. It must be something dangerous because he also ordered the O'Shea brothers to meet us there," Hunter said as he handed her the letter.

"Four Slayers?" Lorena asked.

"Make it five," said DuCassal as he stepped up onto the porch.

Hunter smiled.

"You heard?" he asked.

"Of course. And where you go, I go, mes amis. Besides, we haven't visited that fair city for centuries. I'm curious to see if it has changed very much," DuCassal replied.

"We wouldn't dream of going without you, Jean-Paul," Lorena said as she hugged him.

"Now—where shall we breakfast?" DuCassal asked.

"How about Pere Antoine's?" Hunter suggested.

"Perfect. I am in the mood for a good etouffee omelet this morning," DuCassal agreed.

At breakfast, they discussed the upcoming trip.

"This is the dead of winter up there. The entire region is probably buried beneath several feet of snow and ice. Most likely, even the St. Lawrence River is frozen over. We will have great difficulty reaching Quebec," DuCassal pointed out.

"If we go overland, the trip will take us at least three weeks—maybe even longer. The further north we travel, the more problems we'll have. By the time we reach Quebec, it will be almost spring. That would enable us to reach the city by boat," Hunter suggested.

"Why not take a ship ?" asked Lorena.

"Not many ships risk going up there during winter," DuCassal said. "In the old days, the ports along the east coast were large and busy. Most of the larger ports never recovered from the Great Disaster and remain abandoned to this very day. We could go as far as Charleston by ship. After that, it becomes problematic."

"How about your yacht?" asked Lorena.

"The Bon Chance is very seaworthy, to be sure. But it is mostly a pleasure craft. It's never been on such a journey. It may not make it there and back," DuCassal replied. "But I admit, it would be interesting to try."

"If you're willing, I'm willing," Hunter said. "When can we leave?"

"I can have her ready in one week," DuCassal said with a grin. "That should give us more than enough time to set things in order here before we leave."

Hunter unfolded the second letter. He read it with interest, then passed it to Lorena.

"The Cardinal wrote that the medallion is from an extinct society of knights called the Order of the Dragon," she said. "He also wrote that the order was outlawed in 1500 by the Vatican and disbanded the following year."

"Dracul mean dragon in Romanian," Hunter said.

"Isn't that the name your father assumed when he became a member of the Order?" DuCassal asked.

"Yes. Then he passed it on to me later. He was Vlad Dracul. So my Romanian name was Vlad Dracula. An 'a' was always added to the end of surnames to indicate 'son of' status. It remains that way to this very day," Hunter said.

"Why would Galya [1]slip that into your pocket?" asked Lorena.

"I think a better question is how did she come by it in the *first place*?" DuCassal said. "And why keep it all this time then return it to you in the manner she did?"

"Those are all good questions," Hunter agreed. "And as of now, I have no answers to any of them. Galya never does anything without a reason behind it. But right now, we have more important things to think about. If this medallion is of any real purpose, I'm sure it will be revealed sooner or later."

"And let us hope that it doesn't bite us in the ass *too* hard!" DuCassal smiled.

Quebec.

The two soldiers walked side-by-side through the snow covered cemetery. The night was clear and almost bitterly cold. The men wore

[1] Read "Season of the Witch"

heavy woolen overcoats and fur caps. Even so, they felt the cold almost to their bones.

"This is one freezing night, eh, Marc?" the one said as he shivered. "It's good we only have to be out here for two hours. I can't wait for our relief."

"Me neither, Henri. The sergeant said this was important, but I still don't see the point in patrolling this place each night," March replied as he watched his breath make a steam cloud in front of him. "Let's head back toward the new grave to see if our friends have made an appearance."

They made their way up the winding path to the northeastern corner of the cemetery. The day before, another victim of the mysterious plague had been laid to rest. The last two victims each had been dug up and partially eaten, right under the noses of the guards. Marc and Henri didn't want such a thing to happen on their watch, too.

When they reached the grave, the fresh blanket of snow was undisturbed. The soldiers smiled at each other.

"So far, so good, eh?" Marc said.

"Oui. Our relief should be here in another ten minutes. This will be their headache then," Henri said.

They were just about to turn and walk down the path when the sound of a twig snapping caught their attention. The men froze, unshouldered their rifles and turned in the direction of the sound. A similar sound came from behind them. They glanced at each other and nodded. March faced toward the front while Henri watched their backs. Both had their rifles in the ready position.

But neither was ready for what happened next . . .

Five minutes later, their two replacements walked up the path. As they approached the gravesite, the larger soldier called out.

"Marc! Henri! We are here!" he shouted.

His voice echoed through the night. When no one responded, he readied his rifle. His comrade did the same. They walked slowly up the path and watched the deep shadows every step of the way. They saw no signs of the other two soldiers until they came to a place where the snow and earth had been torn up. They stopped and looked around.

In the middle of the area were two rifles and two fur caps, surrounded by several sets of footsteps. The heavy booted prints had obviously been made by the soldiers. The rest were made by bare feet. And there were several sets of them.

"Marc! Henri! Report!" the soldier shouted.

Nothing.

They walked on toward the grave.

"Sacre Bleu!" the large soldier exclaimed when he saw that the grave had been desecrated.

They walked to the edge and looked down. The coffin was open like the others had been before. And just as before, the corpse inside had been partially devoured.

Ten minutes later, the two soldiers and MSgt. Duchesne were in Montcalm's office. The colonel listened to their report then ordered Duchesne to send out an entire squad to search the cemetery and the surrounding areas for any sign of the missing soldiers.

"Take two of the dogs out with you. Perhaps they may be able to pick up their scent," he said. "Search until I order you to stop."

"Oui, mon colonel!" Duchesne replied.

Montcalm watched them leave and sighed.

This was the first time that two of his men had gone missing. If those things took them, he wondered just where they were taken to and why.

Cpl. Henri Alain Matisse was one of his most reliable men. Pvt. Marc Leonid Chagall had been with the regiment less than a year, but he was well-trained and sharp witted. Montcalm had high hopes for both men and had expected them to rise quickly through the ranks.

Now both were missing.

Taken by those creatures.

"What in God's name are we dealing with out there?" he asked as he looked through his window.

When he reported this to Marquand, the governor general shook his head. This was the first time that soldiers had been taken.

"Should I continue the patrols?" Montcalm asked.

"Of the city and lower towns only. But not of the cemetery," Marquand replied.

"You are just going to allow these things to devour our dead?" Montcalm asked.

"No. I have a better idea. I will issue a decree ordering that all corpses must be cremated from now on. In this way, I hope to deprive those things of their apparent food source. With luck, the lack of nourishment will force them to leave this region to avoid starvation," Marquand said.

Montcalm nodded.

"It seems logical," he agreed. "So far, our visitors have only dined upon fresh corpses. They have not disturbed any of the older graves. But what of the people who have gone missing? We have searched everywhere and have never found a single one of them."

"Continue the searches. Perhaps we may yet discover what became of them," Marquand said.

"We have tried to use the hounds, but this snow prevents them from picking up any scents. Those creatures seem to be very good at covering their tracks. Hell, maybe they don't even leave any," Montcalm said. "I wish I knew what we are dealing with."

"So do I," Marquand said. "In the meantime, continue to search for our missing men. I'll issue the decree this afternoon."

Montcalm nodded.

As he turned and left the office, Marquand sighed.

"I pray to God my plan works," he said.

Savannah.

It was late in the afternoon when Carmello and Riccardo O'Shea returned from their latest house hunting. They were met at the door by their wives, Elizabeth and Kate. The couples had wed the year before after a whirlwind courtship that left the brothers gasping for air. Carmello, or Mel as the locals called him, had married Kate. Riccardo, or Rick, married Liz. They were the teenage daughters of the city sheriff, Bar O'Hara and his wife Maureen.

"How'd it go, Honey?" Liz asked as she gave Rick a big hug and kiss.

"Not so good. We looked at four houses but none of them suited us. I think we'd better start looking for older, larger homes. Perhaps some of the long-abandoned ones might provide what I'm looking for," Rick said as he hung his hat on the peg next to the door.

"I feel the same," Mel said. "I want something very old and large. Preferably haunted like most homes in Savannah."

"But not dangerously so," Rick added. "I don't want a violent ghost."

"What about noisy ones?" asked Liz.

"That depends on how noisy," Mel replied with a laugh. "But the house must be haunted. After all, I don't want the people to think of us as second class because we don't have ghosts."

Liz laughed.

"Let me and Kate look. I'm sure we'll find something," she said. "Oh, by the way, this letter came for you today. It looks important."

She handed Mel the envelope. As he opened it, Rick read over his shoulder.

"It's from the Cardinal," he said.

"Ain't that the guy you work for?" Kate asked.

"It sure is," Rick said.

"What's he want?" asked Liz.

"He wants us to go to the Quebec and assist Hunter with a very urgent matter. He says that the people up there are having some highly unusual problems and have requested our help," Mel said.

"Ain't that up north?" Liz asked.

Mel nodded.

"It's in Canada. That's about a thousand miles from here. I wonder what going on up there and why the Cardinal is sending all of us? It must be really serious," he said.

"And incredibly dangerous," Rick added. "Anyway, it's mid-winter up there. I'm sure the entire region is buried under snow and ice and the rivers have frozen over. The Star of Canada doesn't sail until mid April. Until then, the only way to reach Quebec is by traveling overland. That's not a good idea at this time of year."

"I agree. Right now, we have a small matter to tend to down in St. Augustine," Mel said as he looked through the window at the darkening sky. "There's a storm coming in. It might delay our morning departure."

"We're all packed for the trip. Father Pino didn't explain what was going on down there in his letter. He just said it was urgent. So I packed our entire arsenal. Everything from wood and silver stakes to incendiary grenades and explosive bullets. Whatever turns up, we'll be ready for it," Rick smiled.

Mel laughed.

"If not, we'll improvise like we always do," he said.

St. Francois.

It was two in the afternoon when a weary, snow-encrusted Carl Bergere staggered through the gates of the fort. Another blizzard had struck the area the day after Mayor Lamour told him to go to the fort and tell Pike about the bodies.

Pike and Dr. Norris sat and listened as he related the news. Both knew Bergere very well. He wasn't one to panic over small matters nor exaggerate. Even though what he told them bordered on the bizarre, they knew they could trust his information.

"And you say that Dr. Deaver was certain of this?" Pike asked when he'd finished.

"He was adamant, Robert," Bergere said.

"Mon Dieu! What sort of creature eats corpses?" Deaver asked. "I have never heard of such a thing."

"Neither have I," Bergere said. "Lauren also wanted me to ask if you could patrol the cemetery, just in case whatever did this returns."

"I can spare a man or two. But you'll have to inform me immediately if someone else gets buried there. If that creature likes fresh corpses, I doubt it will return to dig up older ones. The next time someone perishes, I will assign an around the clock watch on the grave from the moment he is buried," Pike said.

"I guess that makes sense," Bergere said.

"As much sense as digging up and eating a fresh corpse," Norris added.

"You've a long, hard trip, mes ami. Why don't you join us for lunch at the mess hall. You can spend the night here if you like. We have several empty rooms in the barracks," Pike offered.

"Merci. I think I will spend the night. I'm too exhausted to return to the village today anyway. We can talk some more over lunch."

As they walked over to the mess hall, Pike wondered what sort of potential nightmare the winter had brought with it.

And there were five smaller villages on Ile D'Orleans. Most were resorts that closed for the winter and the inhabitants usually moved back to their apartments in Quebec. Only Ste. Petronille on the southernmost tip, maintained a year round population. How were they faring?

The guard maintained a small blockhouse there. During the warm months, it was the home to a full squad of 14 men. Only seven stayed during winter. With all of the roads blocked by the snows, there was no way to find out what was going on there.

Pike decided not to worry about them. St. Francois was his only concern for the time being. When the thaw came, he'd send riders to the other villages. There was nothing else he could do right now but wait for spring.

Ste. Petronille.

Sgt. Louis Zender was a 12 year veteran of the Guard. During the winter months, he was in command of the half squad of soldiers who dwelled in the ancient stone blockhouse on the hill that overlooked the picturesque little fishing village.

So far, it had been a harsh but uneventful winter. The men came to roll call each morning and his second, Corporal Jean DeMenil, read off the latest news. Unusually, he had nothing to report and the men were dismissed to tend to daily business.

This morning was different.

Zender watched as his men answered roll call, then turned it over to DeMenil. The corporal looked kind of pale as he cleared his throat and held up the pad on which he logged the daily report.

"I received a message from Msr. Brooks, the mayor of Ste. Petronille," he began. "Msr. Brooks reported that several people in the village have been sickened by a mysterious ailment. This came on them without warning and within hours, all were confined to beds in their homes. The ailment has severe flu-like symptoms accompanied by a high fever. It is not known if this is contagious."

The men stared at each other but remained silent.

"There is more," DeMenil said. "Late last night, the baker, Simon Vey, went missing on his way home from his favorite tavern. The villagers searched everywhere but found no trace of him."

"Is that all, Corporal?" asked Zender.

"Oui, Sergeant," DeMenil said.

Zender stepped forward and looked at his men.

"Until we learn what this ailment is, all of you are hereby confined to the blockhouse," he said. "We have no doctor on duty and I do not want any of you to catch that sickness and share it with the rest of us. That'll be all, men."

"Dis-missed!" DeMenil shouted.

The men made their way back into the blockhouse for breakfast. Zender walked over to DeMenil.

"Both pieces of news are quite disturbing," he said. "Did Msr. Brooks ask for our help to locate Msr. Vey?"

"Not yet," DeMenil said.

"Nevertheless, I think we should pay him a visit this afternoon," Zender decided.

New Orleans

Early the next morning, Hunter, Lorena and DuCassal went over to the old cruise ship pier at the Riverwalk to check out the work being done on the Bon Chance.

The engineman, Larry Beam an, saw them approaching. He put down his wrench, wiped the grease from his hands on his apron and walked down the gangplank to greet them.

"Good morning, Larry," DuCassal said as they shook hands.

"Mornin', Jean-Paul. I just finished givin' her the once over like I do every Monday. What brings you folks here?" Beaman asked.

"Since you know my boat better than anyone alive, I want to ask you a question," DuCassal began.

"Shoot," Beaman said.

"Is she sea worthy?" DuCassal asked.

"The engine needs an overhaul and I have to order a couple of parts, but she'll do for a short trip if you need her," Beaman replied.

DuCassal pursed his lips.

"What's wrong?" Beaman asked.

"Would she be able to make a longer trip?" DuCassal asked.

"How long you talkin'?" Beaman asked.

"Quebec," Hunter said.

Beaman looked at him like he was nuts.

"You're serious, ain't ya?" he asked.

"Very serious," DuCassal said.

Beaman shook his head.

"Not a good idea?" Hunter asked.

"Nope," Beaman said honestly.

"Why not?" asked Hunter.

"She's a pleasure craft, Mr. Hunter. She's built to sail on warm, calm seas and deep rivers. Hell, she only hold a three day supply of fuel at best and rough seas would likely capsize her. Even if conditions were perfect, you'd have to stop every other day to refuel. If she did make it that far, you'd have to steer through all that ice up north. She ain't no ice cutter. She'll never make it," Beaman said.

"That takes care of that idea," DuCassal said as he folded his arms across his chest.

"But we must get to Quebec and the sea is the quickest way to get there. Land routes would take too long and might be impassable the further north we travel," Lorena said.

"Any suggestions, Larry?" asked DuCassal.

"I used to run cargo ships between here and Savannah. As I recollect, a liner called the Star of Canada sails out of there every couple of weeks. That would get you to Quebec. But she doesn't sail until early April when the ice starts to break up on the St. Lawrence River," Beaman said. "That's what I'd do if I were you."

"Could we take the yacht to Savannah?" Hunter asked.

"She'd never make it that far," Beaman said. "The engine leaks oil like a sieve and without those parts, she probably wouldn't get too much further than those old oil platforms out there."

Hunter looked at DuCassal.

"Looks like we'll have to take a commercial steamer into Savannah and book passage on the Star of Canada once we get there. At least that way, we'll be able to take our horses," he said.

DuCassal nodded.

"Well, it was worth a try," he said. "Thanks, Larry."

"I'll get the engine fixed as soon as possible, Jean-Paul," Larry said as they shook hands.

He watched them leave and smiled. He wondered why DuCassal had even asked such a thing since he was the one who designed the Bon Chance. He knew exactly what the yacht was capable of.

He walked back up the gangplank and went back to work on the engine.

"April! That's nearly two months. What if the people in Quebec can't hold on that long?" Lorena asked as they walked over to Bourbon Street.

"They'll have to," Hunter replied. "Even if we went overland, it might take us just as long to get there. Quebec is nearly 2,000 miles from here and it's not an easy trip. Most of the old roads are long gone. Even if we went up the Mississippi, the Great Lakes might also be iced over and impassable. I'm afraid we have little choice but to wait for spring."

"Quebec will still be there when we arrive," DuCassal assured her.

"You hope!" Lorena said.

That night, Hannah Morii was making her usual patrol of the city. It was three a.m. and most of the tourists had already stumbled back to their hotels. As stood in the shadows between two buildings on Bourbon Street, she saw the young waitress leaving her job at the saints and Sinners bar for the day. She was about to walk away when she noticed two rough-looking men emerge from the bar and walk in the same direction as the waitress. Intuitively, she decided to follow them.

The waitress walked over to Burgundy and headed east. The two men hurried their pace. Hannah smiled.

"They are after her," she thought as she silently hurried her pace.

The waitress stopped in front of a Creole cottage between Dumaine and St. Philip. As she fumbled in her purse in search of her keys, the two men accosted her. She attempted to scream but one of them clamped a hand over her mouth while the second man grabbed her arms from behind.

"Just play nice, missy, and you won't get hurt," the first man said.

"Yeah. Now open the door and let us in. After we take what we want, we'll leave. If you go to the cops, we'll be back," the second man threatened.

"If you boys are smart, you'll let her go now and walk away," Hannah said as she stepped out of the shadows.

The men turned.

"Beat it, lady. This ain't none of your business," the first man said as he faced her.

"I'm making it my business," Hannah said as she suddenly grabbed him by the neck.

She had moved so fast that he never saw it coming. The other thug let the girl go and drew a large knife from his belt. Hannah laughed and swung her katana. The man dropped to his knees, screaming in pain and shock as his right hand, still clutching the knife, went sailing across the street.

She lifted the first one off the ground and pinned him against the side of the house.

"You had your chance," she said as she sunk her fangs into his neck.

His partner watched in terror as Hannah drained him of every last drop of blood. When he was totally bloodless, she let his pale, lifeless body slump to the pavement. She turned to the other man and dragged him to his feet. He was now trembling like a leaf.

"Ordinarily, I'd drag you to Basin Street and let Inspector Valmonde deal with you. Unfortunately for you, I haven't fed in a few days—and I'm still hungry," she said.

The frightened waitress watched as Hannah proceeded to drain the life from her would-be attacker. His arms and legs twitched horribly as the blood left his body. Minutes later, he joined his friend on the sidewalk. Hannah wiped the blood from her lips and smiled at the waitress.

"Thanks, Hannah. You showed up at just the right time," the waitress said after the shock wore off. She gave Hannah a hug.

"Who were they?" Hannah asked.

"Beats me. I never saw either of them until tonight. They walked into the bar six hours ago and spent the whole time drinking and checking me out," the waitress replied.

"I'll take them over to Basin Street. Maybe the inspector can identify them," Hannah said. "I guess you're safe now."

"I sure am. Thanks again!" the waitress said.

Hannah hoisted the bodies up on her shoulders and strolled over to the police station. Valmonde was working the midnight shift again. He came out when he saw Hannah drop the bodies on the front steps. She told him what happened.

Valmonde looked them over carefully and shook his head.

"I have no idea who these boys were," he said. "They must be tourists."

Hannah smiled.

"See New Orleans and die," she said.

Valmonde laughed.

"That'd be a good slogan for the tourist bureau. Maybe you oughta run that by them and see if they can use it," he joked.

"Maybe I will when they open this morning," she said as she walked off.

Valmonde laughed and went inside the station. He saw Lem half asleep on a chair and kicked the leg. Lem jumped to his feet.

"Miss Morii left us another gift. Go over to the morgue and tell them to send the meat wagon over for them," Valmonde said.

"Sure thing, Chief," Lem said as he grabbed his hat and hurried out the door.

CHAPTER THREE:
Death Comes Nipping at Your Nose

Quebec, three weeks later.

Montcalm and LeVant were walking along the battlements. It was another cold night and the moon hung pale and lifeless above them. Off in the distance, they could hear the mournful howls coming from the fringes of the surrounding forests. The howls had started several nights earlier. At first, it was just from one or two places. More and more voices joined the chilling chorus until the entire forest seemed to howling with them.

Montcalm pulled up his collar as they looked out over the lower city.

"Listen to those howls in the distance," he said.

"I did not know there were so many wolves around Quebec," LeVant said.

"Those aren't wolves, mon ami," Montcalm pointed out.

"How do you know?" asked LeVant.

"I have heard many wolves howl during my life, Doctor. I can assure you that no wolf that ever walked this Earth ever sounded like that," Montcalm replied.

"The creatures?" LeVant asked.

Montcalm shrugged.

"Either them or some new horror that is about to be unleashed upon the city," he said.

"How far away from the walls do you think they sound?" asked LeVant.

"Sound carries farther on crisp, cold air. I'd say they are several kilometers away. And they seem to be coming from everywhere," Montcalm said.

"Cries of anger for being deprived of their food source?" LeVant asked.

"Or starvation," Montcalm said. "Either way, it is not a pleasant sound."

"No. It is not," Levant agreed.

Since it was getting late, they finished their walk and headed back into the heart of the city. LeVant returned to his apartment above his clinic. Montcalm went back to the Citadel. As long as the things howling stayed far away from the city's walls, he saw no need to worry. Not yet.

An hour after sunrise, Louis Giffe, the caretaker of the cemetery, opened the iron gate and began his daily inspection. It had been nearly a month since the last person was buried here. Marquand's order to cremate anyone who died seemed to have brought the grave desecrations to a halt.

As he strolled along the main path, two mounds of fresh earth caught his attention. They were about one hundred feet from the path, in the older part of the cemetery. He stepped off the path and headed toward the mounds.

What he saw then froze him in his tracks for several seconds.

Two of the graves had been dug up and parts of the rotted coffins, along with gray, decayed body parts were strewn about the area. After he got over his initial shock, he turned and ran out of the cemetery and didn't stop until he reached Montcalm's office at the Citadel.

Montcalm quickly put on his overcoat and ran across the compound to the governor general's mansion and alerted Marquand. Minutes later, he, Marquand and Giffe were in a carriage headed for the cemetery.

"Mother of God!" Marquand exclaimed when he saw the open graves.

There were several long-decayed body parts lying nearby. They had obviously been pulled from the corpses. Some appeared to have been gnawed upon. Marquand was so repulsed by the sight that he spilled his breakfast into one of the open graves.

He composed himself and turned to Montcalm.

"Have some of your men gather up the body parts and take them to Dr. LeVant's clinic. I want him to examine them," he ordered.

Montcalm nodded.

Neither man dared say what was on his mind. It was too terrible to even think about.

LeVant examined the remains and winced while Montcalm and Marquand looked over his shoulder. The bodies were in a very advanced state of decay, which indicated they had been in the ground for years. Most of the flesh had rotted away from the bones long ago, yet the creatures had not only dug them up, they had attempted to eat them. The notion that something was out there that fed on rotted corpses disgusted him to no end.

"Well?" Marquand asked.

"They are like all the others," LeVant replied as he fought down the urge to vomit.

"Mon Dieu!" Montcalm exclaimed.

LeVant nodded.

"Apparently, the lack of fresh corpses has driven those things to this. Even though these bodies barely had any flesh left on them, they were desperate enough to dig them up and eat what little there was," he said.

"Unbelievable!" Montcalm said.

"Just what in Hell are we facing, Doctor?" asked Marquand.

LeVant shook his head.

"Nothing that I ever heard of in my entire life," he said. "I cannot even imagine what they could be or where they have come from."

Marquand sighed.

"Merci, Doctor. You may dispose of these pitiful remains as you see fit," he said as he and Montcalm left the clinic.

LeVant waited until they were gone and ran to the toilet . . .

"Now what, Denis?" Montcalm asked as they walked back to the Citadel.

"We continue to cremate our dead and monitor the cemetery. Any sign of your missing soldiers?" Marquand asked.

"Nothing at all," Montcalm replied.

"Keep searching for them and the others who have disappeared. Maybe we'll get lucky," Marquand said with some resignation.

"And the howling?" Montcalm asked.

"Let them howl all they like—as long as they stay outside the city walls. I want the walls well patrolled each night. Those things must not be allowed inside," Marquand said. "And although most people who live in the parts of the city that lie outside the walls have been staying indoors at night, there are few who venture out for one reason or another. You must also protect them as best as you can."

Montcalm nodded.

All of the people who had gone missing were from places outside the walls. The neighborhoods were large and difficult to patrol, especially with the small force he had at his disposal. And the things always seemed to be able to snatch someone from places where his soldiers weren't. It was obvious that they were watching.

This meant they had some sort of intelligence.

Marquand smiled at him.

"I realize the enormity of your task, mon ami. I know how thinly our soldiers are spread and the vast area they must protect. I also know that it is nearly impossible to cover every part of the city with only 500 men," he said. "Just do your best, as always."

Portneuf.

It was ten p.m. when the soldiers standing watch at the gate saw three obviously frightened villagers rush up to them while shouting for help at the tops of their lungs. Capt. Roche was nearby when he heard their screams and he ran over to see what the commotion was about.

"What's wrong?" he asked the taller man.

All three pointed toward the village while they caught their breath.

"We are being attacked," the man said after a few seconds. "There are creatures in the village."

"How many?" Roche asked.

"We don't know. We didn't stop to count them," the other man said. "We need soldiers—now!"

Roche turned to his sergeant who was standing nearby.

"Arm two squads, Sergeant," he said. "We leave in five minutes."

Five minutes later, Roche and the sergeant were double timing it to the village along with 20 soldiers. When they arrived ten minutes later, a group of villagers, armed with shovels, clubs, butcher knives and pitchforks, met them in the square. Leading was a burly, red-haired man in a fur hat and long overcoat and armed with an old hunting rifle. He was Pierre LeGrand, the village mayor.

"You are too late, Luc," he said. "We've already driven them off. Or at least, I think we have."

"What happened, Pierre?" Roche asked.

"A group of weird creatures came out of the shadows and attacked a couple who were shoveling snow from their front walk. While the husband fought them off, his wife ran down the main street and screamed for help," LeGrand said.

"Everyone who heard her grabbed anything that could be used as a weapon and ran to their house. Just before we got there, several of those things came out of nowhere and all Hell broke loose," he added.

"How many do you think there were?" Roche asked.

"At least ten. Perhaps more. They are hideous creatures, too. Their skin in pale gray, like decayed flesh and are very disfigured and gaunt," LeGrand said.

"Any casualties?" Roche asked.

"They took the husband and two others that I am aware of. Four of us suffered scratches and bites. God, do they smell awful!" LeGrand replied.

"I don't think they bother to bathe very much," another man said.

Everyone laughed.

"They obviously came here to grab some of us. But why? I don't understand," LeGrand said.

"Me neither. Did you manage to kill any of them?" LeGrand asked.

"I shot one of them in his side but it limped off into the woods behind that house across the street. I don't know if it died later," LeGrand said as he pointed.

Roche held up two fingers and pointed. Two me nodded and walked into the woods.

"Are these the same creatures that are eating our dead?" LeGrand asked.

"I would venture to say that it is a good possibility," Roche said as they walked toward LeGrand's house.

"What are they, Luc? Why are they here?" he asked.

Roche shook his head.

"Your guess is as good as anyone, mon ami," he said.

When they reached the house, LeGrand's wife, Lizette, had a pot of hot tea and scones waiting for them in the kitchen. They sat down at the table. Roche poured himself a cup of the tea and watched as LeGrand buttered one of the scones.

"Those things are becoming bold. This is the first time they have dared to attack the village," LeGrand said.

"I'll put more men on patrol around the outskirts after sunset. I'll also need your people to keep their eyes open and report anything unusual as soon as it happens. Even so, we need a faster way of being alerted," Roche said.

"Can your men hear the church bells inside the redoubt?" LeGrand asked.

"Sure. We hear them every time they strike the hour. The sound carries very well, especially on clear cold nights," Roche said.

"Then we can use the bells. Whenever something happens and we need your help, I'll order the bells to be rung. But we'll use a different series of rings so your men won't confuse them with normal hourly rings," LeGrand suggested. "That's much faster than sending runners. Besides, the runners may never make it to the redoubt."

Roche nodded.

"Excellent idea, Pierre. Come up with a signal and sound off at eight tomorrow morning so we can test it," he agreed.

He and LeGrand finished their snack and walked back out into the street. The squads were already assembled in the square. Roche walked over to the sergeant.

"Report," he commanded.

"Our men searched every inch of those woods, sir, but found nothing. There were a few drops of blood but no tracks of any kind. In fact, there was no sign of tracks anywhere in the village other than those of the locals," the sergeant replied.

"Merci, Sergeant. We will return to the redoubt at once," Roche said.

The sergeant saluted, wheeled about and barked orders. The soldiers formed a double line, did an about face, and marched off toward the redoubt.

Roche cursed under his breath in English and French. He turned and shook hands with LeGrand and followed after his men.

LeGrand walked back to his house.

"It has been one Hell of a night!" he thought.

Montreal.

Tomas Bourgue paced his office while Victor Gaude made his end of week report. From what he was hearing, Bourgue decided that it had been a very bad month

Another 44 people had died from the mystery plague. Half had been cremated by their families and placed in vaults. The rest had been buried in the local cemetery. Within three days, each of their bodies had been dug up and partially eaten. To add to the misery, another seven people had gone missing.

Gaude had sent out teams with dogs to search for them, but the deep snow had rendered the animals useless. There were no tracks but those of the missing. Nothing was left behind that indicated where they were taken to.

He turned and looked at Gaude.

"It appears that things are becoming worse, Vic," he said. "It is as if the city is under a siege of some kind by whatever is desecrating our graves."

"What are we facing?" Gaude asked.

Bourgue shrugged and sat down behind his desk.

"No one has of yet seen any of those creatures. We know they strike in the dark of the night when no one is around. They leave no tracks. No clues. It's as if we're being besieged by phantoms. Phantoms who eat corpses and kidnap living people," he said.

"Are any other places experiencing similar problems?" asked Gaude.

"That I don't know, mon ami. With the river frozen and the roads rendered impassable by the deep snows, we have not had any contact with anyone else. Montreal is cut off from the rest of Quebec. Until Spring arrives, we are on our own," Bourgue replied.

"I cannot remember when we've experienced such a bitter winter," Gaude said. "I have heard that for the first time in one hundred years, Horseshoe Falls has completely frozen over. We've even had to cancel the winter carnival this year. That hasn't happened in over 150 years."

Bourgue sighed.

"No one wishes to venture out in such miserable weather and our current circumstances are hardly cause for celebration," he said.

Winter carnival was sort of like a Mardi Gras and was celebrated throughout Quebec, with the largest celebration being in Quebec City itself. The bitter cold and heavy snows had forced just about every city and town in Quebec to cancel the carnival and all but the hardiest souls had remained indoors.

"What are your orders?" Gaude asked.

"Recruit more men for our snow shoveling brigades and do what you can to keep our main streets clear as soon as this present blizzard ends. Since our visitors seem to prefer to dine on fresh corpses, I'll issue an order to have everyone who dies cremated at once. We'll continue the practice for the foreseeable future. Perhaps if we deprive those things of their food supply, we can starve them into leaving," Bourgue replied.

Gaude nodded.

"Good idea, Tom. With no food available to them, they just might leave," he said.

"Or starve to death," Bourgue said. "At the very least, I want to drive them into the open so we can see what we're dealing with and kill them."

"What if they can't be killed?" asked Gaude.

"Let's pray to God that will not be that case, mon ami," Bourgue said with a sigh.

Portneuf

Roche was in his office when Dr. Lewis Marte walked in from the raging blizzard. Roche squinted at him as he kicked the snow from his boots and plopped down in the large, leather chair on the other side of the desk. The doctor looked haggard. Almost worn out.

"And what in the name of God brings you here on such day?" Roche asked.

"Something important, Captain. And horrible," Marte said as Roche passed him cup of hot tea.

"I am listening," Roche said.

"Remember those four people in town who got wounded during the skirmish with those creatures last week?" Marte began.

"Yes. You said they were just very minor injuries. Nothing to be concerned with," Roche answered.

"Well, things have changed. And not for the better," Marte said as he sipped the tea. "What appeared to be very minor wounds began to fester. After two days, they became horribly infected and the men lapsed into deep sleeps. They all had excessively high fevers and sweated profusely while they shivered. I treated them with everything I have at my office. Nothing worked. I thought they were going to die and had Father Murphy prepare last rites.

That's when things got very strange!"

"Oh? Didn't they die?" Roche asked.

"No. Instead of dying as expected, they began to change. The changes were subtle at first. In fact, they were barely noticeable. Then their skin began to take on an almost gray, death-like pallor. Their eyes began to sink in and turn very black and their facial features became twisted. In short, Captain, those men were changing into the very things that wounded them!" Marte explained.

"Mon Dieu!" Roche exclaimed.

"Fearing the worst, we locked them up in a large room so we could watch them closely. They started snarling and howling. And their howls were answered by similar ones from the surrounding woods. Within five days, their transformation was complete. All had changed into those nasty creatures and each began acting violently. I have never seen anything like it before and I imagine that no one else ever has," Marte said.

"Maybe we'd best lock them up in the dungeon," Roche suggested. "We have quite a secure one beneath the redoubt."

"I am afraid that your offer has come too late," Marte said as he shook his head.

"And why do you say that?" asked Roche.

"Those things escaped from the locked room sometime during the night. We have no idea how they got out as the door was still bolted from the outside and the room has no windows. We searched the immediate area and found no tracks leading into nor out of the building. It is as if they had vanished into thin air," Marte said.

Roche sat back and stared at Marte.

The implications were frightening. If those creatures escaped from a locked, windowless room, might they not also be able to enter buildings the exact same way? If so, how would anyone be able to protect themselves from the things?

"Do you suppose that everyone who gets bitten or scratched by any of those creatures will suffer the same terrible fate?" he asked.

"From what we have witnessed with our own eyes, I would say that such a thing must be expected. Now their numbers have been increased by at least four. Perhaps this is also why they abduct people," Marte said.

"If this is true, then we may soon be battling creatures who used to be our friends and family members for control of Portneuf. That is a very chilling thought," Riche said as it sank in. "Very chilling indeed!"

"There is more news, Captain," Marte said. "Ten more people have come down with the virus."

"Does it seem to be contagious?" Roche asked.

"Not that I have been able to determine. It has never been passed to other members in the same households. It seems to be airborne and very random. It strikes young, old, healthy, sick, men, women and even children. Strange though. Not a single child has died from it yet. In fact, those who do contract it seem to fully recover in about eight or nine days. Yet, it's always fatal to anyone over 25," Marte said. "Have any of your men caught it?"

"No. We have been very fortunate so far," Roche said. "Lt. Brande, our regimental surgeon, is keeping a close watch on them."

"Will your men continue to patrol the outskirts of the village?" Marte asked.

Roche nodded.

"I have also double the guard here in the redoubt and placed my company of alert. We'll be able to respond quickly if anything happens again," he said.

Marte rose. They shook hands and Roche escorted him to the door. Marte smiled. It was a very tired smile at best.

"I have experienced 67 winters in my life. This is the worst by far. I'll feel relieved when it ends," he said.

"As will we all, doctor," Roche said.

He watched as Marte walked out into the snowstorm and soon vanished from sight. Roche sighed. His men were trained and equipped to handle every possible emergency and threat to Quebec. But this was something new and almost terrifying.

"When I signed on, I never imagined anything like this," he said.

It was a little past midnight.

Unable to sleep, Roche stayed up to catch up on some paperwork. Halfway through the stack on his desk, he decided to take a break. He poured himself a cup of tea and walked to the window to watch the falling snow. Several more inches had accumulated since the last night and his men had given up trying to clear it from the main pathways.

"Will this ever stop?" he asked himself.

He sipped his tea as he listened to eerie howls.

They were growing louder each night.

Closer.

And they seemed to come from everywhere.

"We are surrounded now," he thought. "Those things are slowly tightening the noose they have placed around our necks. Portneuf is in a state of siege."

He wondered about their recent incursion into the village.

Was that a probe?

Were the creatures testing the defenses and looking for signs of weakness?

If so, that meant they were organized and perhaps intelligent. That would make them even more dangerous to deal with.

The sudden frantic clanging of the church bells snapped him out of his thoughts. He put down his tea cup, strapped on his pistol belt and grabbed his overcoat and hat as he rushed out onto the parade ground.

His men had already assembled in four squads. He drew his pistol, checked to make sure it was loaded, and led his men out of the redoubt and down the road to the village at a dead run . . .

It was an hour after sunrise when the battle ended. It had been a wild, chaotic melee. The creatures had entered the village from five directions and attacked anyone they saw on the streets. The men again responded with pitchforks, axes and the few hunting rifles they had. The battle was already raging when Roche and his men entered the fray. That's when the creatures ceased going after the villagers and turned their full attention to Roche's soldiers.

The five hour running street battle ended when the sun rose and the creatures melted back into the shadows like wraiths, leaving at least a dozen villagers and soldiers dead, more wounded and six missing. Two dozen lifeless creatures lay amid the human dead as well.

Roche and the mayor, Pierre LeGrand, surveyed the aftermath.

"It looks like we've chased them off again," LeGrand said.

"I think they retreated because the sun was rising. I don't think they like moving about during daylight. Anyway, this appeared to be an attack in force," Roche said. "They seemed to be everywhere."

They stopped to examine one of the dead creatures lying in the street. It resembled a desiccated corpse and was clad—if one could call it that—in tattered slacks and the remains of a loose checkered shirt.

"What in God's name is that?" LeGrand asked as Roche turned it over.

"I doubt that God had anything to do with the making of this creature," Roche said. "At least now we know they can be killed. They are not invulnerable. This one died from a head shot."

"I'll have my people gather up all the bodies and burn them. Even our own dead. I don't want these things feasting on their remains," LeGrand said. "What about the wounded? You know what happened to the others."

"Strap them into their beds and watch them closely for any signs of change. If any of them look like their turning into one of those things, I suggest you put them out of their misery before it's completed," Roche said.

"You want us to kill our own people?" LeGrand asked. "Isn't that kind of harsh?"

"I think that's better than allowing them to become one of those monsters," Roche replied. "I'm going to do the same with any of my men who may have been injured. The last thing we need is more of those creatures to contend with later."

LeGrand nodded.

"This stinks, you know that, don't you?" he said.

"To high Heaven," Roche agreed.

He bade the mayor adieu and marched his weary soldiers back to redoubt. After joining them at the morning mess, he trudged back to his office and hung his overcoat on the peg. That's when he noticed a sharp pain in his left calf. He sat down, removed his boot and saw that his trousers had a long rip in them. He rolled up his pant leg and winced when he saw the jagged scratch.

He cursed and rolled his pant leg down. He then slipped on is boot and overcoat and limped over to the dispensary to see Lt. Brande.

Brande cleaned and dressed the scratch.

"Was this made by one of those creatures?" he asked.

"I'm not certain. I don't recall any of them getting close enough to injure me. I may have scratched myself while running through the streets. I really don't know," Roche said as he adjusted his clothing.

He saw the expression on Brande's face and nodded.

"I know what you're thinking. I am thinking the same thing. Keep close watch on me, Doctor. If I show any signs of change, you have my permission to lock me in one of the dungeon cells for my own safety and the safety of the men. In fact, I'm making that a standing order," he said.

"And as the second ranking officer, you will be in command of this redoubt. I know you have the combat skills and training necessary to handle the position, so I will not be missed," he added after some thought.

"I hope it will not come to that," Brande said.

"Me, too," Roche smiled. "How many of the men were wounded?"

"Two," Brande said. "Only two. But two have gone missing."

"I am afraid that they will return to plague us shortly," Roche said."

The Vatican.

The Cardinal was in his office trying to choke yet another horrid meal prepared by his well-meaning but hopelessly inept cook. Each time he put a forkful of the strange mess into his mouth, he silently prayed that once it hit his stomach it would have the decency to remain there until it could be digested.

He was about to put yet another morsel into his mouth when a knock on his door mercifully interrupted him. He dropped the fork back onto his plate and pushed it aside as Fra. Capella entered bearing a strange box wrapped in plain brown paper and tied with string. The Cardinal smiled and motioned for him to sit down.

Capella placed the package on the desk.

"This arrived just a few moments ago, Excellency," he said. "It's addressed to you."

"I can see that," the Cardinal said as he pulled the box toward him.

Capella watched as he cut the strings with the knife from his lunch tray and peeled away the paper. When he opened it and looked inside, he wrinkled his brow.

"What is it?" Capella asked.

The Cardinal turned the box upside down and emptied the contents onto his desk. Several pieces of wood fell out along with a small note. Capella stood and studied the pieces. He watched as the Cardinal reassembled them into a small wooden crucifix. Both men cast puzzled looks at it.

"Why would someone send me a broken cross?" the Cardinal asked.

"Perhaps the note will answer that," Capella suggested.

The Cardinal nodded. He unfolded the note, squinted, and passed it to Capella. The Friar scratched his head.

"Manus Dei?" he asked.

"Hand of God," the Cardinal translated.

"I know. But what does that have to do with a broken cross?" Capella asked.

"I don't know, but I want you to do whatever you can to find out. Someone sent this here for a reason. It's a signal or threat of some kind. I need you to find out what it means," the Cardinal said. "Start with the Archives. Compile a list of every organization that has ever been associated with the Church. Go as far back as you can. Once you have that, try to find out which organizations still exist and for what purposes."

"I'll get right on it, Excellency," Capella said. "One more thing: Hunter wrote and advised us they will take a steamship out of Savannah in early April. That should place them in Quebec in time for spring thaw."

"I wonder what they will find there," the Cardinal mused.

Portneuf.

Roche now burned with a fever. It had started the night before and progressively worsened. He ached all over and his stomach churned and had to be emptied almost hourly. As he again staggered to the toilet, he stopped to look at reflection in the mirror above the small sink.

It was not a pleasant sight.

His skin was taking on a decidedly gray tint and his eyes had sunken in. His fingers were becoming rough and gnarled and light bothered him.

He heard a knock at his door.

"Entres vous!" he called out.

Brande entered and stopped in his tracks when he saw the changes in his friend.

"My God, Luc! You look like death itself!" he remarked.

"I know. I feel it is almost time to transfer command to you. I want you to lock me in one of those cells no later than tomorrow evening. I'll write a letter to officially relinquish command. That way, you won't have to answer so many questions," Roche said.

Brande nodded.

He realized there was no other way. He'd already confined the other wounded men to dungeon cells after they'd reach the point of no return. At least Roche still maintained control of his mind and personality. But the changes were inevitable. Like the villagers.

"I'll prepare a comfortable room for you, Luc. You should be able to move in after the morning meal," he said.

"Merci, mon ami. I will dress and join you and the men for one last inspection of the redoubt. I'll pull my collar up to conceal some of the changes from the rest of the men," Roche said as he pulled on his heavy boots.

"They already know of your condition, Luc. They understand what is happening and they have seen the changes in the others. Although they are worried, they show no signs of panic or fear," Brande assured him.

Before Roche could respond, the unmistakable and frantic sounds of the church bells echoed through the redoubt.

"Damn! Not again!" Roche said as he strapped on his pistol belt and reached for his overcoat. "Assemble the men!"

Brande rushed out to carry out his orders. As Roche put on his fur hat, he cursed under his breath.

"Once more into the breach," he said as he opened the door and ran outside.

When Roche and his men reached the village, the battle was in full bloom. Women and children were screaming and running in all directions while their men struggled to hold off the army of creatures that had emerged from the woods and other dark places. Roche deployed his men in two columns and they made a slow, steady sweep of the village. The creatures saw them and, instead of fleeing as they had before, they instead charged straight at them. Rifle shots echoed through the streets and alleys along with the shouts and screams of dead and dying. The battle raged until the first rays of sunlight peaked above the mountains in the east and the creatures retreated into the shadows.

When it was over, the streets were covered with dead villagers, soldiers and dozens of the creatures. Pools of blood stained the snow and more than one house was burning out of control.

Roche looked around as his men staggered back into formation. He looked at Brande.

"Report, Lieutenant," he said.

Brande saluted.

"We have five dead and seven missing. At least six more are wounded," he said.

"How many villagers are dead?" Roche asked.

"I don't know, mon Capitan. The mayor is still assaying the damages," Brande said.

Just then, a rather ragged and dirty Pierre LeGrand, along with at least 50 villagers, trudged into the town square.

"How bad were you hit, Pierre?" Roche queried.

"I'd guess we lost about 100 people. This is one battle we'll not soon forget," LeGrand said.

"This was no battle, mon ami. It was a nightmare," Roche said. "This situation has become untenable. The village cannot be adequately protected from those things and I do not have enough men to fight more such battles."

"What do you suggest?" LeGrand asked.

"I suggest that anyone who desires to be evacuated to Montreal should gather up whatever they can carry and return to the redoubt with us. Those who have their own means of transportation should leave the village as soon as possible," Roche replied.

"I'll get the word out," LeGrand assured him.

Two hours later, Roche and his soldiers, along with nearly 300 villagers, trudged into the redoubt. LeGrand had decided to remain behind to help gather up and cremate the corpses. He said he try to make it to Montreal in his own boat later.

Roche watched as his men escorted the villagers into the two empty barracks buildings and sighed. He now felt himself changing by the minute and had to use all of his willpower to maintain his personality. He knew that was likely his last action at the head of his soldiers. Soon, he'd become just another one of those creatures and be condemned to gorge upon corpses for the rest of remaining days.

Brande walked up and saluted.

Roche managed a grin.

"I think we can dispense with such formality, mon ami," he said. "See to it that everyone is fed and care for sick and injured as best as possible. I'll be in my quarters."

"Shall I prepare you cell?" asked Brande.

"Give me a few more hours. I think I still have some time," Roche said as he walked to his quarters.

St. Francois.

Norris walked into Pike's office and sat down. Pike looked up from his breakfast tray and nodded.

"Good news or bad?" he asked.

"Terrible," Norris replied.

Pike put down his fork and leaned back.

"I am listening, Herbert," he said.

"All three of our stricken men took turns for the worse last night. I did what I could with what we have in the dispensary, but it wasn't enough. All four passed away just before dawn. I am sorry," Norris said sadly.

Pike sighed.

"Have them buried with full honors in the cemetery outside the walls. I'll have Sgt. Roget gather up their personal effects. I'll have them sent to their families along with letters of regret. What was it, Herbert? What killed them?" he said.

"I wish I knew, Bob. At first, I thought it was influenza. But they grew too weak too fast," Norris said.

"Examine the rest of the men on a weekly basis. If anyone else shows the same symptoms, quarantine him at once. I don't want our entire company wiped out," Pike said.

"Have you heard from the men patrolling the cemetery in town?" Norris asked.

"Oui. They returned an hour ago. They reported that all was quiet last night. I'll send two others tonight," Pike said. "Has the disease spread to the village?"

"I am afraid that it has. Dr. Deaver told me that there are at least seven such cases right now," Norris said. "I imagine that they'll be digging seven graves shortly."

"I wonder if any of those will also be dug up." Pike said.

"Whatever did it earlier is probably still lurking nearby. Since it did it once, it's a safe bet to say that it will do it again. Animals always return to their hunting grounds," Norris said.

"What makes you so certain that it is an animal?" asked Pike.

"What else could it be, Bob?" Norris reasoned.

"I hope you're right, mon ami. If it isn't an animal, I shudder to think of the other possibilities," Pike said.

"Like what?" asked Norris.

"Have you ever read any of the old Lovecraft stories?" Pike asked.

"Of course I have. He is one of my favorite writers. Why?" Norris answered.

"Think of what he wrote about. Especially in the story called 'Pickman's Model'," Pike said.

Norris raised an eyebrow. He knew exactly what his friend was suggesting. The idea that such creatures actually existed repelled him. He shook his head and laughed.

Pike scowled.

"It's as good an explanation as any," he said. "Think about it, Herbert."

"I'd rather not, if you don't mind," Norris said.

Portneuf.

Roche smiled weakly as Brande locked the cell door from outside.

"This will do nicely," he said. "It has all of the comforts of home, provided one lives in a prison."

Brande laughed.

"I wish there were some other way," he began.

"But there isn't," Roche said. "I have some last orders for you and I want you to carry them out at your earliest convenience."

Brande nodded.

Roche sat down on the cot and looked up at him.

"Have Sgt. Delavega take half the men and escort the villagers to Montreal. We have six longboats at the dock. That should be enough. The ice has started to break up so they should be able to reach Montreal safely if they are careful," he said. "Do it tomorrow if you can."

Brande nodded.

"And the rest of us?" he asked.

"Maintain the defense of the redoubt for as long as possible. If the situation becomes untenable, you are to abandon this post and retreat to Montreal. I have put both orders in writing. They are on my desk," Roche said.

He saw the expression on Brande's face and smiled.

"Only a fool tries to hold onto something after it is lost. To Hell with this redoubt, Perry. The safety of our men must be your only priority. If those things overrun the redoubt, I say let them have it. Just get the Hell out of here," he said. "And that is my final order."

"What about you and the other men?" Brande asked.

"If we are still in these cells when you abandon this redoubt, I want you to put a bullet through each of our skulls. I'd rather be dead than become one of those creatures. I'm sure the other men feel the same way," Roche said.

"You have my word, Luc," Brande promised.

Quebec.

It was one a.m. and the Vieux Port was deserted save for the two soldiers patrolling it. Their path took them along Dalhousie toward the terminal where several of the larger fishing boats were moored.

During the warmer months, Vieux Port bustled with tourists, shoppers, fishermen and locals. It was the busiest section of the city. Now, in the dead of winter, it was as silent as a crypt. It had been virtually devoid of life since the first snowfall.

The soldiers laughed and joked with each other as they walked. After all, nothing ever happened in this part of the city. It was over two miles from the nearest cemetery. The patrol was merely a normal part of their nightly routine.

As they strolled past Barricade, they stopped and waved at the three men on the walls. The men waved back and they exchanged the usual insults. They all laughed.

All was quiet on the docks.

The men on the ramparts relaxed. One leaned against the stone wall and lit his pipe. As he puffed it to life, they heard two distinct, explosive sounds. The soldier dropped his pipe.

"Gunshots!" he shouted. "They came from the port!"

Within seconds, every soldier within earshot was scrambling down the ice-covered steps and hustling toward the docks. When they reached the location the shots had come from, all they found were two rifles, two fur hats and a canteen in a leather case. The two soldiers were gone.

One of the men spotted an odd, pink stain in the snow. He knelt to examine it as the others gathered around.

"I think this is blood," he said as he stood.

"Fan out and search the area. They have to be here somewhere," the ranking corporal ordered. "I'll run and tell the Colonel."

Montcalm wasn't very happy being roused from his sleep at two a.m. He was even less happy with the corporal's news.

"Have the bugler sound the alert. I want every man and hound out searching for them within ten minutes," he ordered as he slipped on his boots.

But try as they might, his men found no traces of the missing soldiers nor their abductors. Even the bloodhounds failed to find any traces they could follow in the snow. At sunrise, Montcalm called a halt to the search and ordered his men back to the Citadel for a hot meal. After they were fed and rested, he'd send out another search party.

But the men, he knew, would never be found.

When he told Marquand, the Governor-General stared. The implications were very clear.

"They are growing bolder. Too damned bold," he said. "You said there was a blood stain?"

"I believe it is blood. It is blood-like but very pale. Sort of anemic looking," Montcalm answered.

"That means our men shot one," Marquand said. "Did he kill it?"

"That I cannot say, Denis. There was no body or tracks of any kind. Only that one stain. I must assume the creature was only wounded," Montcalm replied.

"I want you to double the patrols in the port. The weather seems to be braking lately. Once it warms up a bit, we'll be able to put more men out at night," Marquand said.

Montcalm nodded.

"I have already issued the order," he said. 'Those things are forcing us to cover a wider and wider area. It is as if they are trying to stretch us too thinly to protect the entire city."

"We must assume we are dealing with intelligent creatures who are capable of studying our defenses and able to plan ways to get through them. If they are not, then we must assume there is a higher intelligence guiding their actions. Either way you want to look at it, it is not very pleasant," Marquand said.

"Oh, one more thing, Denis. My men tell me that the ice in the eastern part of the river has started to break up. It should be passable within a few weeks," Montcalm said.

"Maybe then those people Challons sent for will be able to reach us," Marquand said. "Have you heard from Levis?"

"Not a word," Montcalm said. "Nothing at all since the river froze."

"I pray to God they are not experiencing similar troubles," Marquand said.

"So do I, Denis. So do I," Montcalm agreed.

New Orleans.

It was a typical rainy night. The kind of night where the rain drove most of the tourists into bars or hotels and the streets were mostly deserted. Around two a.m., Hunter and Lorena walked into the Dragon, the main vampire club in New Orleans. The owner, Tony LeFleur, was tending bar and he waved when he saw them. They sat down at their usual table and waited while Madison hustled over with their drinks.

"How's it going, Madison? Bite anyone lately?" Hunter joked.

She laughed.

"Not lately. Nobody's pissed me off for a while," she said as she sat down with them. "I heard you're going up to Quebec."

"Who told you that?" asked Lorena.

"Jean-Paul of course," Madison said.

"Of course!" Hunter smiled. "It's true. We're being sent up there by the Vatican. Something strange is going up there and he wants us to take care of it."

"When do you leave?" Madison asked.

"In early spring. The St. Lawrence River will start thawing by then and we'll be able to reach the city," Hunter said.

"I've never been to Quebec. What's it like?" Madison asked.

"I haven't been there for a long, long time," Hunter said. "It was quite beautiful then but things change."

Tony left the bar and sat down with them.

"My ancestors came from Quebec. They left after the British took over. They settled in a small town called Ste. Genevieve for a few years then moved down here to New Orleans. That was before 1800," he said. "Most of us Cajuns originally came from Nouvelle France as it was called back then."

"I, too, have never been to Quebec," Lorena said. "I'm looking forward to seeing it."

"I went up there about 10 years ago. You'll love it," Tony assured her. "Why is the Vatican sending you?"

Hunter shrugged.

"The Cardinal didn't elaborate. He's also sending the O'Sheas out of Savannah," he said.

"Must be something really nasty if he's sending five of you," Tony said. "How long will you be gone?"

"I have no idea. A month or more," Hunter replied.

"You will be missed," Tony said.

"I'm sure Hannah and Alejandro can handle anything that comes up while we're gone," Hunter said. "New Orleans will be in good hands."

Quebec.

Marquand paced his office as LeVant brought him the latest news. It was grim to say the least. Montcalm and Duchesne were also in attendance. Each had a report to make. Neither liked what they heard from LeVant.

"We've had seven more cases of that strange virus this week. So far, all of the infected patients are still alive. Two may be gone before tomorrow morning as they are already spitting up blood when they cough. That makes 23 such cases in the last two weeks. All but these seven have died," LeVant said.

Marquand stopped pacing and looked at LeVant.

"Do you have even the slightest idea what this disease is, Doctor?" he asked.

LeVant shook his head.

"I have never seen the like of this in all my years of practicing medicine. It has a 100% kill rate. That makes it the deadliest disease in human history," he said. "Luckily, it seems to spread very slowly."

"That is small consolation," Marquand said as he sat down.

"I agree," LeVant said.

"And what have you to report, Colonel?" Marquand asked.

"Even though we are cremating our dead, the older graves are still being dug up and the corpses are being eaten," Montcalm said. "I have added more men to the nightly patrols, especially within the city walls and the port. So far, no one else has been attacked. Those creatures seem to be content with the bodies for now."

"But they may not stay that way for long," Duchesne interjected. "This morning, one of my patrols found sets of footprints just outside the north walls. There were four distinct sets and they appeared to be walking along the base of the remparts."

"That means they are looking for a way into the city," Marquand said. "Tell our men to be doubly alert from now on. I don't want any of those things to get inside. Add more patrols to the areas immediately outside the walls and keep warning everyone who lives out there to get home before dark and to keep their doors and windows locked."

He looked at LeVant.

"Any word from Challons about the help he requested?" he asked.

"Bruno informed that he received a letter from Msr. Hunter yesterday informing him that he and his party will depart New Orleans on the 12th—which was yesterday. It will take them at least two weeks to get to Quebec. Their ship makes stops in St. Augustine, Charleston and a couple of other ports along the eastern coast," LeVant replied.

"Just who is this Hunter?" asked Marquand.

"According to Bruno, he is the top Slayer of the Vatican," LeVant said. "His wife and best friend are coming with him. Two other Slayers will join them later after they complete an assignment in St. Augustine. The Vatican must think this is a highly dangerous situation to be sending us five Slayers."

Marquand nodded.

"The more, the merrier, eh?" he smiled.

"I am glad the good Father has requested such help. I must admit that is far beyond anything me or my soldiers have ever had to deal with before. Fighting corpse-eating monsters is not within my field of expertise," Montcalm said.

"Or mine," Marquand agreed.

CHAPTER FOUR:
The Uncooperative Dead

St. Augustine

Antonio Lopez was the current alcalde or mayor of the ancient city. He stood five feet ten inches tall, had jet black hair and a neatly trimmed goatee. Like most of the residents of St. Augustine, he preferred to dress in the manner of colonial Spaniards. He'd been the mayor for the last ten years, mostly because no one else wanted the job.

Earl Justinian Potter was the police captain. He and his men wore the uniforms of Colonial Spanish soldiers and were quartered in the ancient fortress known as Castillo de San Marcos. Potter kept his head clean shaven and looked like a brawler. He had a force of 48 men, which was more than enough to police the sleepy, usually peaceful city. In an emergency, he could call up an addition 125 reserve officers. Twenty two of his men were mounted police.

Padre Emilio Pino was the city's religious leader. He held mass each Sunday at the ancient Cathedral Basilica. Pino handled all the baptisms, communions, last rites and acted as a family counselor when needed. He also performed most of the weddings in the area. It was he who had written to the Vatican requesting help. The Cardinal immediately forwarded his letter to the O'Sheas.

It was late afternoon when the steamship came up the Intracoastal Waterway and docked at the marina. The three men watched as the passengers disembarked. Mel and Rick were easy to spot, thanks to their distinctive black leather coats and wide brimmed black hats.

Lopez stepped for with his hand extended and made the introductions as Mel and Rick shook hands with them. They then followed the men up Charlotte Street a few blocks, then crossed Plaza de la Constitution to the old Government House where Lopez had his office.

A cute young woman with dark smiled and greeted them as she made a pot of coffee.

"This is my daughter, Alicia," Lopez introduced.

They went into his large office and sat down at his desk. Alicia brought in a pot of coffee on a tray with several ceramic mugs and placed it before them. She left and returned with a pile of small sandwiches she had made.

Lopez poured each of them a mug of coffee. Rick drank his, picked up a sandwich and sat back.

"Tell us what's going on here that requires our services," he said.

Lopez looked at him and sighed.

"Over the last several months, we have experienced a string of highly unusual deaths here," he said. "These are not of natural causes. Nor were they standard kinds of murders one might expect to have here once in a while."

"As the police captain here, I have seen a fair number of murders. I've seen stabbings. Shootings. A poisoning or two and even a person hacked to bits with an ax. But I have never seen anything like these. Nor has anyone else I dare say," Potter added.

"These deaths are very strange and mysterious. That's why I wrote to the Cardinal and asked for help. I feel that we are dealing with something supernatural that only men like you can handle," Pino said.

"How many deaths are we talking about?" asked Mel.

"There have been 27 deaths over the last six months," Lopez replied. "Each died the exact same way."

"And just how *did* they die?" Rick asked.

"They all appeared to have been drowned," Lopez said.

"Drowned? You mean they died at sea?" Rick asked.

"No. They drowned in their homes. In their beds," Lopez said.

Mel raised an eyebrow.

"What do you mean?" he asked.

"Each person was found in his or her bed by family members the next morning. Both the victims and their beds were soaked with seawater and there were even bits of seaweed here and there. Yet none of the victims had been out on the ocean the day before," Lopez explained.

"Autopsies revealed that their lungs were also flooded with seawater. In effect, each had been drowned while lying asleep in their beds," Pino added.

Rick whistled.

"The first victim was found the morning after we celebrated the 2,700th anniversary of the founding of St. Augustine. Since then, there has been one murder each week," Potter said.

"No wonder you've asked for help," Rick said. "People drowning in their own beds on dry land certainly fits into the realm of the supernatural."

"Anything else?" Mel asked.

"Yes. Each victim had one of these in his mouth," Pino said as he took a silver coin from his pocket and passed it to him.

Mel turned it over several times while examining it and tossed it to Rick. Rick looked it over.

"This is a very ancient French coin. I'd guess that it was minted sometime during the early 16th century of the First Age," he said.

"Exactly. That would place it at about the same time frame that St. Augustine was founded by the Spanish," Pino said.

"But why a French coin? What connection does this have to St. Augustine?" Rick asked.

"That goes back to the early years of the colony," Pino said. "In 1562, a large group of Huguenots arrived in Florida and established a colony which they called Fort Caroline. They consisted of mostly French soldiers and were led by Jean Ribault.

So, actually, they had arrived here three years earlier than the Spanish.

Those were brutal and dangerous times. Spain, France, England, The Netherlands and Portugal were all trying to establish control over the New World. Anyone who tried to stand against them, was put to the sword. Spain took the harshest measures possible and were especially brutal toward the natives, whom they looked upon as heathens and savages. In fact, they worked most of them to death.

The religious wars and prejudices of Europe were now transplanted to the Americas and carried out with a vengeance. No one knows how many millions were slaughtered as neither side bothered to keep a count. They just kept fighting each other until it was no longer profitable.

In 1565, Ribault decided to drive the Spanish out of Florida. He gathered a small fleet and attacked the numerically inferior Spanish garrison at Fort Matanzas. But a storm rose up and destroyed the French fleet. The survivors, including Ribault, staggered ashore and attempted to surrender to Captain Pedro Menendez de Aviles. As a condition for surrender, Menendez ordered the Huguenots to convert to Catholicism and swear fealty to the King and Queen of Spain. Ribault and his men refused so Menendez put them to the sword and tossed their bodies into the ocean. He had every last one of them killed and that's how the fort got its rather bleak name.

Matanzas means massacre in Spanish."

"Interesting. What happened to Ft. Caroline?" Rick asked.

"The Spanish wiped it off the map a year later. The Huguenots were allowed to remain as long as they swore to serve Spain. They might have been massacred, too, if not for the intervention of the Catholic priests here," Pino said.

"Where was Ft. Caroline?" asked Mel.

"It later became known as Jacksonville after America took control of Florida. It's nothing more than a pile of swampy ruins right now. It was destroyed and abandoned during the Great Disaster," Pino said. "No one lives there now."

"Are you sure?" Mel asked.

"This is Florida. No one can ever be 100% certain of anything," Lopez said with a grin. "Except heat and death."

"The Huguenots were not allowed to be buried in Catholic cemeteries. For many years, they were interred with the Natives outside the city limits. In 1821, the Presbyterian Church established the Huguenot Cemetery in St. Augustine to bury all of the non-Catholic victims of a yellow fever epidemic. The last interment there was in 1884," Pino said.

"Fascinating. And each drowning victim had one of these ancient French coins in his mouth?" Rick asked.

Lopez nodded.

"There has to be a connection between what happened at Matanzas and the drowning," Rick said. "Or at least someone or something is trying to show us they're connected. Do any of the descendants of the original Spanish colonists still live in St. Augustine?"

"Most of us can trace our lineage back to 1565 when Menendez arrived," Lopez said with a touch of pride. We even have an annual ball to commemorate our heritage."

"And the murders began right after that," Mel smiled. "Now I *know* there's a connection."

"But the massacre occurred in 1565. Nothing of the kind has happened here until lately. Why the long wait?" asked Lopez.

"That's the part we need to figure out," Rick said. "Are there any legends attached to this incident?"

"A few. The waves that roll onto the beach at the site of the massacre turn blood red on each anniversary. I've never seen that happen, though. Locals say the ruins of the fort are haunted by the spirits of the Huguenots. And, according to the local lore, Ribault swore he'd return from the grave to avenge the massacre no matter how long it took. But that's never been substantiated," Pino said.

"What exactly did he supposedly say?" Mel asked.

"One legends has it that he'd come back to strike down everyone who had anything to do with the massacre even if it took forever," Pino said.

"I think we may have something. How far back do your birth records go?" Rick asked.

"They go back to the founding," Pino said. "They are very meticulous up until 1885, then they get kind of murky for some reason."

"We need to have a look at them. We also need a list of every victim associated with this case," Rick said.

"No problem. Stop by the church tomorrow. We keep all those records in the archives there," Pino offered.

"I'll provide the list of the victims," Potter said. "Tomorrow morning soon enough?"

"That's perfect. We'll check into the hotel tonight then take a walk around the city. We'll see you at the church tomorrow," Rick said as they shook hands.

"We set you up in a suite at the Casa Monica. It's our best hotel," Lopez said. "Alicia will show you how to get there."

Portneuf.

It was nearly 11 the following night and a light snow was tumbling to the Earth to add to the thick, white blanket that was already on the ground. Brande was in the office going over the day's paperwork.

It had been a busy day, too.

The villagers and half of his men had boarded the long, flat boats early that morning. By now, he thought, they should be in Montreal. Safe from the madness that permeated Portneuf. The rest of his men—all 44 of them—were in full alert. There were still a few dozen people left in the village. Those who could, left for Montreal. But in every such situation, there were always those who refused to leave their precious homes behind. Even the mayor had decided to stay. He was unwilling to cede their ancestral homes to the creatures.

A knock at the door broke his train of thought.

"Entres!" he called.

He nodded as Sgt. Lorimeir entered and saluted. Brande returned it.

"What's on your mind, Robert?" he asked.

"I have just returned from the cells, Sir. They are empty!" Lorimeir said.

"Empty?" Brande asked.

"Oui, sir! Completely empty. Yet the doors were locked from the outside and the bars on the windows were still in place. It is as if the man vanished into thin air," Lorimeir said.

Brande sat back and looked at him.

"That will be all, Sergeant," he said.

Lorimeir nodded and left the office. Brande shook his head.

"Bon chance, Luc—wherever you are," he said sadly.

That's when he heard the church bells echoing through the night. He jumped up and grabbed his gear.

"Here we go again!" he said as he ran out to his already assembling soldiers.

St. Augustine

It was eight p.m. The streets of the old city were now dark save for the glare of the gas lamps. Mel and Rick decided to patrol the oldest part to familiarize themselves with St. Augustine. As they walked along St. George Street, they passed Smokey Joe's Café. A sign in the window caught their attention.

"Are you brave enough to risk Damnation?" it read.

"What do you suppose it means?" Mel asked.

"Let's go in and ask," Rick suggested.

The café was a long, narrow affair with a counter in back and small kitchen behind it. There were about a dozen small tables. They walked in and sat down. The place was empty save for the man behind the counter and a small, cute blond-haired waitress who rushed over to greet them.

"We saw the sign," Rick said.

"What's it all about?" asked Mel.

"That's our food challenge," she said.

"Food challenge?" asked Rick.

She nodded.

"We have a sandwich called the Damnation. We say it's the hottest sandwich on Earth and we challenge anyone to eat it," she said.

"What does one get for doing so?" Mel inquired.

"You get a t-shirt that says "I survived Damnation", you get the meal for free and we put your names up on the wall of fame," she replied as she pointed to a brass plaque above the counter.

They saw that there were only three names on the plaque.

"Three out of how many?" asked Rick.

"Fifty," she said.

"What exactly is on the Damnation?" he asked.

"The sandwich is a foot long and has a pound of marinated roast beef, hot pepper cheese and a sauce made from 12 ghost peppers, four scorpion peppers, two Carolina Reapers, and habaneros. You have to finish every bite of it in 30 minutes to win the challenge," she said. Then she winked at them.

"Do ya'll have the nerve to try it?" she dared.

They looked at each other.

"I'll try it if you'll try it with me," Rick said.

"Agreed," Mel said. "Bring us two."

"I hope you boys know what you're getting into," she said as she walked back to the counter.

They watched as she told the cook. He looked at them and smiled.

"Are ya sure?" he called out.

The both nodded.

"The worst thing that can happen is we end up in a doctor's office," Rick said.

"Or the morgue. I can see it now. Our epitaphs would read: At least they tried," Mel joked.

The waitress brought the sandwiches to their table. Then she and the cook and two customers who had come in while they were waiting, sat around to watch. Mel took a deep breath and eyed the sandwich.

"The best thing to do is eat it as fast as we can and avoid the burn," Rick suggested.

Mel nodded.

The waitress looked at her watch and counted down. When she reached the number one, she yelled, "Go!"

They dug right it and started wolfing down the murderous meal. Almost from the beginning, beads of perspiration broke out on their foreheads and their eyes began to water. After a few hearty bites, Rick complained that he could no longer taste anything or even feel his tongue. Mel said he could feel the wax inside his ears melting and wondered if he still had a tongue. With each bite, the fire inside their mouth and their stomachs grew hotter and hotter.

Halfway through, Rick put the sandwich down and raised his hands in surrender. Mel tried bravely (or foolishly) to carry on but threw in the towel two bites later.

The waitress brought over two large glasses of cold milk. They downed them quickly. The milk only seemed to make things worse.

Mel took several deep breaths, which fanned his internal flames. He looked at the waitress.

"You said only three people have succeeded?" he asked.

"That's right," she said.

"I take it then that two of them had their t-shirts draped over their coffins prior to being buried?" Mel asked.

"Something like that," she answered with a giggle.

"Actually, no one has died that I know of. Most just wish they were dead afterward," the cook said with a grin.

Mel handed him $20 for the tab. R. got up and bolted for the toilet around the corner, where he spent several minutes puking up what felt like the live coals from a furnace. It felt like lava was erupting from his mouth and he was bathed in sweat from head to toe. He heard Rick pounding on the door.

"Find your own toilet!" he shouted as he stuck his head in the bowl and emitted a horrifying sound.

Mel dashed outside. He threw up in patch of grass. The vomit actually made the grass and earth smoke when it touched them.

R. staggered from the toilet looking as pale as snow. His entire body felt as if as engulfed by fire and his heart raced out of control. He looked at the waitress.

"I guess we failed miserably, huh?" he asked.

"You got further than most," she said.

"Somehow, that does not serve to console me," he said as he tipped his hat and went outside to find Mel.

He found him two streets away, leaning over the side of a fountain with his face in the water. He walked over and sat down on the edge of the fountain. Mel lifted his head from the water and looked at him.

"If Hell has 666 levels, then that sandwich is surely from the 665th!" he said. "Every pore of my skin is sweating acid now. Even my tears and snot burns when I sneeze. I didn't think I could experience anything like this and survive."

"I'm not so sure we've survived yet," Rick said as he handed Mel his hat. "My entire body is trembling out of control right now. I'm going into some sort of internal shock."

"Let's return to the hotel. At least that way, we'll both be close to a toilet," Mel said as they walked up the street.

As soon as they entered their suite, Rick charged into the bathroom. Me heard liquid splashing into liquid followed by a loud moan. Ricks staggered out and plopped down on the sofa. He looked up at his brother.

"Even my piss burns like fire," he said. "I'm afraid of doing the other."

"One thing is certain. Neither of us can have any sort of germ or bacteria left alive in our bodies. We have been purified by fire tonight," Mel said.

Rick laughed then felt something rising up within his stomach. He doubled over in pain and forced himself to his feet. Mel watched him rush into the toilet again and laughed. A few moments later, he found himself in the other toilet with his head in the bowl.

St. Francois.

Pike stood on the parade field in front of the redoubt with several of his soldiers. The sun had set less than an hour ago and the full moon above was partially obscured by moving clouds. Soon after the sun set, the night became filled with eerie howls that emanated from the distant forests that surrounded St. Francois.

Pike shivered.

Partly from the chill in the air.

Partly from the way those howls made his spine tingle.

"What in God's name is making that sound?" one soldier asked.

"Those are just wolves," another suggested, although he didn't really believe that.

"No wolf ever sounded like that!" another soldier said.

Pike listened.

The howls sounded plaintive and mournful.

Painful.

They almost had a human tone to them.

"What do you think they are, mon Capitan?" asked the first soldier.

Pike shrugged.

"That I cannot say, private," he said. "I have not heard the likes of it before."

"They give me the creeps," said one soldier.

"Don't let them get to you," Pike said. "For now, it is just a sound in the night. It's nothing to fear."

The soldiers nodded.

Pike smiled.

"Carry on as usual. If anything changes, come and get me," he said as he took his leave.

They watched him walk toward the barracks.

"The Capitan is right. Whatever is making those sounds is miles away from here. I think we are safe—for now," one soldier said.

"But what of tomorrow night?" another asked.

He laughed.

"Worry about that tomorrow," he said.

When Pike reached his office, he found Dr. Norris waiting for him.

"Allo, Herbert. What do you think is howling out there tonight?" he asked as he sat down at his desk.

"All I can say for certain is they are not wolves," Norris replied. "I've written the death certificates for each of those poor men. The rest is up to you."

Pike looked at the papers on his desk and sighed.

"Those were young, tough men. How could they have succumbed so quickly?" he asked.

"I can't tell you that, Bob. Hell, I don't even know what killed them. I've arranged for the burial detail tomorrow. Are you sure you don't wish to reconsider my suggestion?"

"I'm sure. They will be buried with full honors as is our custom. Why do you want to cremate them anyway?"

"Isn't that obvious?" Norris asked.

Pike looked at him.

"You really think those things will try to dig them up?" he asked.

"Oui. It has already happened at the village cemetery. Why should it not happen here?" Norris replied. "There is something out there that feeds upon the recently deceased. Perhaps it is the very same things that are howling out there now."

"Lovecraft?" he smiled.

"Perhaps there is more truth in his writings than anyone suspects," Norris said. "He did have a habit of vanishing for days, even weeks at a time. Then he'd show up at August Derleth's home looking like death warmed over. After a few days of rest, he started writing. Who knows where he'd gone or what he'd seen? Lovecraft never said."

"You make this sound as if we are just characters in some sort of horror novel!" Pike joked.

"What if we are?" Norris challenged.

"Now you are being absurd!" Pike scoffed.

The howls were also heard in the village. As soon as they began, most of the villagers came out of their shops and homes to listen and argue about what was causing it. Just about everyone had a different opinion and the debates lasted well into the early morning hours.

In the clinic, Dr. Deaver looked over the charts of the latest group of villagers to come down with the strange ailment.

There were four.

Three men and one woman.

All fluctuated between teeth chattering chills and burning fevers.

They had been brought in the night before. Deaver had admitted tem immediately and began treating them with everything he had his disposal.

As expected, nothing worked.

They just grew worse.

Just like the others.

He sighed in despair as he notated their charts and passed them to his nurse, Agatha. She looked at each and nodded. Deaver had written only one word on each.

"CREMATE"

He left the clinic and walked over to City Hall to tell Lamour the latest news. He would try to get her to pass an official decree ordering the cremation of anyone who dies for the foreseeable future.

"If those things want to eat bodies, they will have to go elsewhere to find them," he said.

CHAPTER FIVE:
Strangers in the Night

St. Augustine

Mel and Rick walked over to the Cathedral the next morning. They both still felt a bit under the weather. Pino laughed when they told him of their ordeal or as Rick put it, "Our trial by fire." Pino led them down into the basement where the archives were stored and unlocked the ancient iron door with a large, iron key.

"The records start with the shelf to the right and go all the way around the room. They each cover the births and deaths of a ten year period. Before I forget—" he reached into his pocket and took out a folded sheet of paper. He handed it to Mel.

"Here's the list of all of our drowning victims. Captain Potter sent it over this morning just before you arrived. Good hunting!" he said.

They delved into the ancient tomes with all of the energy they could muster. As they did, they worked backward, using the names from Potter's list and looking for links to St. Augustine's founding families.

After four hours, Rick sat back and rubbed his eyes.

"It's just as we suspected," he said. "Each one of the victims had a lineage that dates all the way back to 1565. But in each case, there are no male descendants left to carry on the family name. All of their lines have been broken."

"There might be something to Ribault's curse after all," Mel said.

"We can't rule that out. The thing that gets me is how does one drown in one's own bed? Lopez said their lungs were filled with sea water and their beds were soaked as well," Rick said.

Mel shrugged.

"The connection is the French were thrown into the sea after they were butchered. Some may have been alive at the time, so they drowned. This is obviously some sort of payback. As for the bed part, maybe they were dragged from their homes, drowned and placed back in their beds—which doesn't seem likely since no one saw or heard anything. Or---" he said.

"Or what?" asked Rick.

"I don't know where I was going with that," Mel admitted.

"You're no help," Rick said.

"I never claimed to be," Mel reminded him. "But when dealing with the supernatural, anything is possible."

"I'm too tired to read anymore today. At least we've gotten what we came for. We've established a definite connection between the murder victims and the original Spanish settlers. It seems the Spaniards kept very meticulous records just to make sure they got property inheritances correct. We've also established that each victim's ancestor had been a Spanish soldier under Menendez's command," Rick said.

"And Ribault swore that he'd avenge the massacre of his soldiers no matter how long it took," Mel said as they got up and walked upstairs and into the apse.

"If that's all true, why'd he wait so long? What caused him to return now?" Rick asked. "We're no closer to the answers than we were last night."

"We need help, Padre," Mel said when he saw Pino.

"What kind of help?" the Padre asked.

"We need to speak with someone who knows all of the local paranormal lore and legends," Rick said.

Pino nodded.

"I know just the man!" he said.

St. Francois.

Pike, Norris and most of the men in the company stared in horror at the dug up graves of their recently buried brothers in arms. The men had been buried with full honors only two days earlier. The desecrations were discovered when Norris went for his daily walk through the small cemetery.

Pike crouched at the edge of the nearest grave and shook his head. Never in all his years as a soldier had he seen anything like this. Each grave had been excavated. Each coffin had been broken into. And all four of the bodies had obviously been eaten to some extent.

Sergeant. Roget and two of the men walked up and saluted. Pike stood and returned their salute.

"There are no tracks anywhere, Sir," Roget said. "None leading into or out of the cemetery."

He looked around.

The entire cemetery was still covered by several inches of snow.

"What you are telling me is impossible, Sergeant," he said. "Nothing on this Earth can move through snow without leaving tracks. Nothing!"

"We scoured every inch of ground, Sir. I swear there are no tracks," Roget insisted.

"He's right, Bob," Norris said. "Look around the graves. There are no tracks at all."

Pike nodded.

"Have some men gather up what is left of the bodies and take them to the crematorium in the village. The rest of you cover up these graves," he said.

He and Norris walked back into the redoubt.

"Now do you believe me?" Norris asked.

"I don't know what to believe anymore, mon ami," Pike replied.

"This is exactly what happened in the village," Norris said. "They found no tracks, either. It's like we're dealing with phantoms."

"Phantoms who devour corpses," Pike added. "That leaves me with 43 men still fit for duty—unless you have more bad news?"

"No. The rest of the men are healthy and fit," Norris said. "I check on them daily. The ailment does not seem to be contagious."

"Well, that is at least one small bit of good news, eh?" Pike said with a half smile. "From now on, we will cremate everyone who dies. Those things must be deprived of their source of food."

"Now you're seeing it my way," Norris said. "Better late than never."

"Smart ass!" Pike joked.

"You notice there was no howling last night?" Norris asked.

"Oui. Now I know why. They were too busy feasting on the bodies of our men," Pike said as the entered his office. "I guess they only howl when they are hungry, eh?"

"So it appears," Norris said as he hung up his overcoat. "But exactly what are we dealing with? No animals that I know of do that. Not even the hungriest of wolves dig up graves and eat corpses."

"I feel as if I'm trapped in a nightmare," Pike said as he poured them each a cup of strong coffee. "But who's?"

It was then they heard a knock on the door.

"Entres vous!" Pike called.

The door creaked open and a tired-looking Bergere entered. Pike saw the expression on his face and knew he didn't come on a social visit.

"What can I do for you, Carl?" he asked.

"Something strange happened in the village last night, Bob. Lauren wants you to look into it," he said.

"What?" Pike asked.

"A young couple went missing just before midnight. They were on their way home from a dinner party at a friend's house. When they didn't show up by sunrise, the woman's mother reported it to the mayor," Bergere said.

"Did you send out searchers?" Pike asked.

"Of course. But they found nothing. Nothing at all. Not even tracks. They are just gone!" Bergere replied.

"I will send a squad out with two bloodhounds this afternoon. Perhaps the dogs will be able to pick up their scent," Pike said.

"Merci, Bob. I'll inform Lauren," Bergere said as he hurried out of the office.

Pike looked at Norris.

"This just gets stranger," he said.

Sgt. Roget and the squad arrived at the village two hours later. Bergere escorted them to the house the couple had last been seen at. Within seconds, the dogs picked up their scent. The trail led halfway to the couple's house then suddenly stopped. The dogs circled and sniffed for several more minutes but found nothing. Roget had his men fan out in all directions while he stood back with the dogs and waited.

He smiled at Bergere and the woman's mother who were standing nearby.

"They are the best trackers in all of Canada. If anyone can find them, they will," he said.

An hour later, his tired squad came drifting back. Sadly, they had nothing to report. Roget sighed and shook his head. The woman sobbed and went back inside her house.

"I am sorry, Monsieur," Roget said. "Truly sorry."

"You and your men did all you could, Sergeant. Merci," Bergere replied.

He watched as the soldiers and dogs marched back toward the redoubt. When they were out of sight, Bergere pulled his collar up and headed back to City Hall.

When he reported the results to Mayor Lamour, she glared at him.

"That's impossible! There has to be tracks somewhere. People just don't vanish into thin air. They simply don't," she said.

"*They* did," Bergere said. "There's no trace of them at all. It's like they've been plucked from the Earth by an unseen force."

"I want you to form another team. Go back there and keep searching. I want them found, Carl. I want them found soon," Lamour said.

Bergere nodded.

He did as she instructed. He formed a team of 23 men, mostly good hunters and trackers and sent them out in search of the couple. After a full day and night of searching, the team gave up and returned to City Hall.

The young couple were never seen again.

St. Augustine

John Bartholomew Harper was one of the few remaining Timucua Indians in the area. It was his ancestors who greeted Ponce de Leon when he arrived in Florida in 1516. There were about 145 Timucua left and they lived in their original village of Seloy at the site of the Fountain of Youth Park.

They had reclaimed their homeland two years earlier and the local authorities saw no reason to stop them.

Harper was the tribal shaman and chief. He stood nearly seven feet tall and had jet black hair tied into a single brain in back, broad shoulders and a narrow waist. He was seated in front of his cabin when Rick and Mel rode up.

"I know why you've come here," he said as he eyed them with interest. "The spirits told me all about you. You want to know why this is happening now instead centuries ago."

"Right. Why would Ribault wait so long to exact his revenge? What event triggered this?" Mel asked.

Harper smiled.

"Those are good questions," he said.

"Do you have any answers?" Rick asked.

"Not offhand. I think the place to begin your search would be the site of the massacre. Have you been to Matanzas?" Harper asked.

"Not yet," Mel replied.

"There isn't much left of the fort now, but you might get lucky and find clues amid the rubble," Harper suggested.

"How do we get there?" asked Mel.

"By boat," Harper said.

"We don't have a boat," Rick said.

"But I do," Harper smiled. "I'll take you there now if you like."

"Let's go!" Rick said.

CHAPTER SIX:
The Ancient City

Quebec.

It was early on a Tuesday afternoon in late April when the captain of the steamship, Star of Canada, deftly navigated through the chunks of floating ice that still partially blocked the St. Lawrence River.

Hunter, DuCassal and Lorena stood on the upper deck with the other passengers, admiring the snow covered landscape of the surrounding hills and islands. Here and there, patches of green and red roofs could be seen peering out of the snow and wisps of smoke rose out of the chimneys.

Normally, the ice and snow would be gone by this time of year. But this had been an unusually long and harsh winter. One that clung stubbornly to the region and refused to leave without a fight.

As they pulled into the landing dock, Lorena studied the city. She could see that it was ancient and the architecture resembled some of the older regions of France. The lower part of the city was protected by a small stone fort that was, like the rest of the walls, in remarkably good condition.

Hunter pointed to the fort.

"That's Batterie Royale," he said. "I was the commanding officer there. It looks pretty much the same as it did then. So does the rest of the city."

"Except for that huge structure standing above the ramparts, Charles. That was not here in those days. That came over a century later when the Canadian Railroad built it to be the grandest hotel in all of North America," DuCassal said. "I invested in it back then. The return on my investment was more than a hundred fold. It's too bad you weren't around back then. But I did use some of the money to maintain your home in New Orleans. I knew you'd return one day and I wanted you to feel comfortable."

Hunter laughed.

"What's it called?" Lorena asked.

"The Chateau Frontenac," DuCassal said. "It's quite magnificent."

"Is that where we'll be staying?" she asked.

"No. I have had us booked at our old favorite. It is the oldest hotel in Quebec," DuCassal replied with a grin.

"Not Auberge du Tresor!" Hunter said.

"The one and only. I have a single room for myself and a suite for you and Lorena," DuCassal said. "I thought you wouldn't object."

"You thought right, Jean-Paul. Thanks," Hunter said as he patted him on the back.

As they drew closer, they could see several uniformed soldiers on the walls of the Batterie Royale as well as the muzzles of several small artillery pieces. Hunter knew the Batterie was able to hold a dozen such guns. Eight cannon and four heavy mortars.

"The lower city is called Place Royale," he said. "It was the first place settled by French explorers and traders in 1608. The upper city sprang up soon after and was walled in to protect it from attacks."

"How many times was it attacked?" she asked.

"Six. The first four times was by the British. The last two was by the Americans. That's why the Citadel was constructed by the British during the 1820s. It was to deter any further attacks from American forces," DuCassal said.

Hunter thought that city still looked to be under siege. But, he wondered, just who or what was besieging it?

"What do you think, Lorena?" he asked.

She smiled approvingly.

"It's beautiful. Even under all that snow and ice, it looks very romantic. No wonder you and Jean-Paul enjoyed coming here," she said.

"Those were the grand old days, eh, mon ami?" DuCassal said as he fondly recalled how they'd conducted business with the Quebecois and Hurons before it fell to the British in 1759.

The fur and copper trade had been hugely profitable for them in those days, as had their many other ventures. It seemed that everything they did turned to gold for them. Cotton. Rice. Coal. Iron. Rum and even wine.

Hunter smiled and nodded.

"The best," he said.

Marquand stood on the dock and watched as the steamship slowly slid up. Two crewmen jumped out and moored the ship to the dock with heavy ropes. When it was secured, other crewmen lowered the gangplank. There were 17 passengers aboard. Hunter and his friends were easy to sort out.

"Welcome to Quebec," Marquand said as he extended his hand. "Msr. Hunter, I presume?"

Hunter shook his hand and made the introductions.

"Where are you staying?" Marquand asked.

"We've booked rooms at the Auberge du Tresor," DuCassal said. "It was our favorite hotel when we visited Quebec many years ago."

"Excellent choice. We can go there in my caliche. I'll have your horses and luggage brought to you later this afternoon," Marquand offered.

"It has been many years since we were in Quebec," DuCassal said as they walked to carriage and climbed in.

"I am sorry that your return visit is not under more pleasant circumstances, Msr. DuCassal," Marquand apologized. "But please try to take advantage of our famous hospitality while you are here."

"I'm sure we will," Hunter smiled as he looked out upon the old familiar streets.

"This is my first visit to Quebec. I am anxious to see it," Lorena said.

"I promise that you will love it here, Madame. Everyone does," Marquand said with more than small hint of pride. "There is no other place like Quebec anywhere else on Earth."

Later that afternoon, they met with Marquand, Montcalm, LeVant and Fr. Challons in the Governor-General's office at the Citadel. Montcalm explained the events that occurred over the last few months. The descriptions of the desecrated corpses made Hunter wince. When he finished, Hunter leaned back in the chair.

"We can rule out werewolves," he said. "Werewolves don't eat dead bodies. They're hunters and killers. They prefer live prey."

"That's exactly what I've been saying all along," Montcalm said. "Loupgarou aren't carrion eaters, so these creatures must be something else entirely. Something that has never been seen before."

"But they have also attacked and killed living people. At least, I must assume they have been killed," Marquand added.

"What do you mean?" asked Hunter.

"Several people have gone missing. In fact, nine went missing in the last ten days, including two from the unit," Montcalm said. "There's no traces of them anywhere and we have never found any of them."

"There were seven men and two women. All were taken between midnight and daybreak. That's when most of the kidnappings occur," Challons added.

"When my men were taken two nights ago, we heard the shots they fired. They were patrolling the Vieux Port. By the time I got there with a squad of soldiers, all we found were their hats, rifles and bits of clothing. The only tracks in the snow were those of the missing men. Those creatures never leave tracks of any kind," Montcalm said. "So far, I have lost four men to those things and we are no closer to learning what we are dealing with."

"This just gets stranger and stranger," Hunter said.

"Indeed it does, mon ami," DuCassal agreed.

"At first, only the most recently buried were desecrated. Since we stated cremating anyone else who dies from the plague, they have started digging up older graves," Challons said.

"That sounds like they're becoming desperate. There aren't any fresh corpses around to satisfy their hunger so they're scavenging for anything that's even remotely edible. Whatever they are, they may be on the verge of starvation," Hunter said.

"What happens when they run out of corpses altogether?" asked Montcalm.

"Use your imagination. What would you do if you were them?" Hunter asked.

"Mon Dieu!" Challons exclaimed.

"Exactly," Hunter said.

"You make this sound hopeless!" Marquand said.

"No. It's not hopeless. Not yet. First, we have to figure out just what we're up against. Then we have to find out where they've come from and where they take their captives," Hunter said.

"Then what?" asked LeVant.

"We kill them," DuCassal said with a smirk.

"We are dealing with creatures that prowl at night. They devour corpses and kidnap the living. I have never heard of such things, mon cher," Lorena said.

"Neither had any of us until this nightmare began," Challons said. "Now you know why I've asked the Vatican for help."

"And why the Cardinal sent every Slayer he had in this part of the world," Hunter said.

"There are only three of you?" Marquand asked.

"For now. Two more will arrive when they've completed an assignment in St. Augustine. That's all of us," Hunter said. "That should be enough."

"You can rely on my soldiers to be at your side, Msr. Hunter. We have been in the thick of this mess since it started. I see no reason for us to step aside just because you are here now," Montcalm assured him.

"The Home Guard is made of the toughest, best-trained soldiers in all of Quebec. Each man is worth ten ordinary soldiers in any given situation. That's why it is alarming to have any of them taken by those creatures," Marquand added.

"Have they ever attempted to get past the walls?" Hunter asked.

"Not yet. I think they fear the walls," Montcalm said. "So far, they have confined their incursions to the cemeteries and the outskirts of the lower and upper city. The Vieux Port is the closest they have ever come and even that was too close."

"I'd like to have a look at your defenses," Hunter said. "Can you give us the grand tour?"

"I would be honored to," Montcalm said. "When would like to do it?"

"How about now?" Hunter asked.

"I am at your service, Monsieur," Montcalm said.

They left the hotel and walked down Sainte-Famille to the Remparts. Hunter smiled at the array of cannon and mortars and thought back to the first time he had seen them. They walked to the walls and looked out over the Vieux Port.

"It's just as I remember it," he said.

"Yes, it is, Charles," DuCassal agreed.

"After the world collapsed around us, the Governor-General at that time decided it would be wise to reconstruct the original fortifications and arm the city with every available artillery piece. It proved to be a most excellent decision. These walls have saved Quebec time and again over the centuries," Montcalm said with obvious pride.

They followed the remparts south. Every few feet, they stopped while Hunter examined the defense works and checked the guns. Along the way, they encountered several highly alert guards who saluted Montcalm smartly. He returned it and bade them to carry on.

"How many men are on guard during daylight?" Hunter asked.

"Twenty-four. There are two on each gate and the rest patrol the walls and the areas below," he replied. "At dark, we double the number."

"Have you had any trouble during the day?" Lorena asked.

"No, Madame. Everything happens at night," Montcalm said.

They continued their inspection until the passed the Citadel. They stopped just north of it. Hunter leaned on the wall and looked out upon a vast, open area of pure white snow.

"The walls are in excellent condition. They're just as they were the last time Jean-Paul and I inspected them the night before Wolf's army appeared on the Plains of Abraham," Hunter said as they stopped a hundred yards south of Porte St. Louis, which was one of four main, fortified gates leading into the old city.

Montcalm stared at him.

"But that was over 2,000 years ago," he said. "That means both you and Jean-Paul are immortal!"

"We are," Jean-Paul assured him. "If we have expiration dates, I am unaware of it."

"We were officers under your ancestor. We came up here during the Seven Years War to help defend the city from the British. We've never had any particular love for them anyway. We had just beaten them in several battles. Montcalm thought he had driven them off. Then we learned that Wolf's regiments had scaled the cliffs to the west of the city," Hunter said.

He looked out upon the snow covered Plains of Abraham and imagined Wolf's regiments lining up in battle formation.

"Jean-Paul, Montcalm and myself stood on this exact spot watching them. There were 3,000 crack British troops. All were infantry as they had no way of carrying artillery pieces up the side of the cliffs with them. I remember smiling because I knew there was no way on Earth they could take the city with rifles and bayonets. If they attacked the walls, they'd be slaughtered like sheep by our artillery and muskets," he said.

He turned and looked Montcalm in the eyes.

"That's when the general informed us of his plan to march out and meet the British on the Plains," he said. "Jean-Paul and I argued against this. We told him it was madness to meet them in the open. We had less than half their number and only 600 of our men were professional soldiers. The rest were just local militia without much experience. We pleaded with him to stay behind the walls and let the British attack them at their own risk. We told him they could never take the city by storm. The attack would fail and the British would withdraw from Canada as they had before."

"But he refused to listen to reason," DuCassal added. "He did not trust the fortifications for some reason known only to himself. So we marched out to meet the enemy on the open Plains. Wolf arrayed his soldiers in a new battle formation that allowed for enfilading fire. Montcalm studied their lines. Then, to our amazement, he ordered a frontal assault."

"The rest you know. We did hit their lines despite suffering heavy losses. We fought with valor and determination and nearly carried the day. But a British musket ball found its way into Montcalm. We broke off the engagement and carried him back into the city, leaving the field to the British. At almost the same time, one of our men managed to shoot Wolf. Both men died hours later without ever knowing the outcome of the battle," Hunter said.

"The defeat demoralized the city. Although we still held a strong, fortified position and could have driven the British off, the city magistrates opted to surrender. Jean-Paul and I along with hundreds of others migrated to the Louisiana Territory rather than remain under British rule," he added.

"How sad. Perhaps if my ancestor had heeded you advice, history would been much different in this part of the world," Montcalm mused. "Was that the last time you visited Quebec?"

"No. We returned over a century later as officers in Benedict Arnold's expeditionary force when he tried to wrest control of the city from the British during the American Revolution. We damned near succeeded and might have if Arnold didn't have his knee shot out from under him. We actually got inside the city for a little while. It was nearly an improbable victory," Hunter said with a smile.

"So you are of French extraction?" Montcalm asked.

"I am," DuCassal said. "Charles is more Romanian."

"I've always wanted to return to Quebec. I never imagined it would be under these circumstances," Hunter said.

Montcalm nodded.

"Believe me, sir, when I say that no one in this entire city ever imagined there would be such circumstances," he said.

"What can you tell me that you know for certain?" Hunter asked.

Montcalm shrugged.

"The only thing I can say with any kind of certainty is that those things seem to be increasing their numbers. And, judging by the sounds of the howls they make each night, I'd say they are coming closer to the city. We used to hear only a few howls and they came from a great distance. Tonight, you shall hear them for yourselves," he said.

"Any idea of their numbers?" Hunter asked.

"Dozens, at least. Perhaps hundreds," Montcalm replied. "For now, they are staying beyond the lower remparts. But I fear they may become bold enough to attack if they feel they outnumber us," Montcalm said.

Hunter looked out at the island in the distance just as a bank of fog rolled in to obscure it.

"That's Levis, isn't it?" he asked.

"Oui," Montcalm said.

"Have they had any trouble with these things?" Hunter queried.

"I do not know. We have not had any contact with Levis since the river froze. Now that the ice is breaking up, I plan to visit the town tomorrow afternoon. Would you like to come along?" Montcalm asked.

"Yes, I would," Hunter said. "What about other places? Have these things appeared anywhere else?"

"I truly cannot say," Montcalm replied. "We usually lose contact with most places each winter. That's when our roads become impassable because of the heavy snows and the river freezes solid for several weeks. This winter has been especially long and harsh. I haven't heard from anyone since the first blizzard struck over four months ago."

"Are the other places defended by your soldiers?" DuCassal asked.

"We have reduced companies at Portneuf Redoubt, Fort Stewart, Montreal and some smaller outposts. I have 932 men on regular duty," Montcalm said.

"What's the nearest?" Hunter asked.

"Portneuf. It is about 86 kilometers from here," Montcalm said. "I normally station 200 men there. Before winter sets in, I reduce their force to one company."

"What about supplies?" Hunter asked.

"The redoubt is self-sufficient. They hunt and fish most of the year and grow or purchase other necessities from the nearby village. When winter arrives, they always have more than enough food and medical supplies on hand to last until spring. The meat is stored in the post ice house and the other things are canned," Montcalm explained.

"How large a place is it?" Hunter asked.

"About one quarter the size of the Citadel," Montcalm said.

"When was the last time you heard from them?" asked Lorena.

"Right before the first blizzard struck Quebec," Montcalm said.

"That's nearly five months. Is that unusual?" Hunter asked.

"Sometimes when the winter snows hit, all of the roads become impassable and the river freezes solid. That cuts off all contact between here and other places. During winter, we have little or no communication with any other places. It is the price we pay each year for living up here," Montcalm said.

"How far up does the river freeze?" DuCassal asked.

"From Quebec City all the way up to and past Montreal. This winter was particularly cold and snowy. In fact, we got over 40 feet of snow this year. At one point, it snowed for 23 consecutive days," Montcalm said.

"Did those things show up right after the first blizzard?" Hunter asked.

"Oui," said Montcalm. "As I recall, the first desecration occurred less than a week after."

"Do you know if they've attacked other places?" Lorena asked.

"I have no idea, Madame," Montcalm replied. "As I have explained, we were snowed in all winter. But when the ice and snow began to thaw last week, the incidents intensified."

"Interesting," Hunter said.

"Very," DuCassal agreed.

"After we visit Levis, I think we should go up to Portneuf," Hunter said.

"We came up river this morning," DuCassal said. "So the ice is breaking up. We should be able to reach Portneuf without too much trouble."

"I agree," Montcalm said. "As you have come all this way to assist us, I have decided to allow you to, as you say, call the shots. I am a career soldier. I am trained to fight human opponents. These creatures are way outside of my realm of expertise."

They continued their inspection of the fortifications. They stopped when they arrived at Porte St. Louis. Hunter looked out at Parliamentary Hill. The ancient government buildings still stood and the fountain still bubbled as it always had.

"The walls look as strong as they ever were," Hunter observed. "Stronger."

"Over the centuries, we have rebuilt and even improved upon the original designs. We even restored four of the gates," Montcalm said with a touch of pride.

"Can the city withstand an attack?" Lorena asked.

"Of course it can, Madame," Montcalm assured her. "Provided we have enough soldiers to man them. These days, that might prove to be a problem."

"How so?" Hunter asked.

"I now have 500 men on active duty at the Citadel. They are the finest soldiers in all of Canada and well equipped. If those creatures decide to attack Quebec in one spot like they did just before you arrived, we can easily beat them back," Montcalm replied with a slight swagger.

"What if they attack in more than one place?" Hunter asked.

"Then we have a problem," Montcalm replied honestly. "My 500 men are not enough to cover all six kilometers of the fortifications. There would be large gaps in several places where my men would be spread very thin. We'd have to know exactly where and how many troops to send to a given area in an instant's notice and hope we get there in time. We've trained for such contingencies, of course. But that is not the same as doing it for real."

"What about reserves?" DuCassal asked.

"There are some retired soldiers I could call to duty. I'm not sure how many we have. My best estimate is about 450," Montcalm said.

"Do you have enough weapons in the armory to supply them?" Hunter asked.

"Oui. We always keep an extra 1,000 rifles on hand. We keep them in excellent working condition, too. It's become a tradition," Montcalm said.

"Who can issue an activation order?" Hunter asked.

"Denis," Montcalm said. "Only the Governor General has that power. Why?"

"I think it's time to call up the reserves," Hunter said.

They returned to the Citadel and entered Marquand's residence. A butler showed them into his office. The Governor-General greeted them warmly then sat back as Hunter offered suggestions and made his request to call up the reserves.

Marquand listened then shook his head.

"I do not feel it is necessary to activate any of our reserves at this time," he said.

"Might I ask why not?" Hunter queried.

"Such a call up might instill the people of the city with a sense of panic. I would prefer to avoid doing that for the time being," Marquand replied.

"I understand," said Montcalm.

"I don't," said Hunter.

Marquand looked him in the eyes.

"The reserves are only called upon in times of emergency," he explained.

"And you don't feel this is an emergency?" DuCassal asked.

"Not yet," Marquand replied.

"Then what would you consider an emergency?" asked Hunter.

"An attack inside the wall of Quebec," Marquand said. "Once they show they can enter the city and breach our defenses, I will call up the reserves."

"In that case, I hope to Heaven that you never have to call up a single soldier," Hunter said.

"And if you do, pray that it is not too late," DuCassal added as they left his office.

Outside, Hunter growled in frustration.

"Is he always this unreasonable?" he asked.

"You must understand where Denis is coming from, Msr. Hunter," Montcalm said.

"You do?" Hunter asked.

"Oui. That is why I did not pursue the matter further," Montcalm said.

"Do you agree with it?" Hunter asked.

"Not entirely but he is my commanding officer and I will carry out my orders to the best of my abilities," Montcalm said with a sly grin.

"You are a true professional, Colonel," Hunter said.

"Most of the time, anyway," Montcalm said. "I do not tell Denis everything unless I feel it is important. He usually leaves most of the military matters to me. He has enough on his plate governing Quebec."

Montcalm smiled.

"His opinion is not without merit. He was the commanding officer of the Guard for many years. When he retired, the command passed to me," he explained. "Outside of a few minor skirmishes with would-be pirates and marauders up north, the regiment has not seen much action of late. Our men constantly train and learn new tactics. Yet I feel this current situation will truly test us."

"What does the Guard normally do?" asked Lorena.

"For the most part, we act like a police force, Madame, except in Montreal which still maintains a small force of Royal Canadian Mounted Police. We also conduct patrols of the northern frontiers and patrol the river during warmer months," Montcalm said.

"So there's no police department in Quebec City?" Lorena asked.

"No. Long ago, it was decided that paying to maintain both a police force and a military force was redundant. So the police department was merged with the Home Guard and we assumed the normal police duties. In times of trouble, we are a crack military regiment. In times of peace, we are the police," Montcalm explained.

"That makes perfect sense," DuCassal said.

"Yes. It does," Hunter agreed.

"Have the Quebecois always been so practical?" Lorena asked.

Montcalm laughed.

"Only when it comes to spending the taxpayers' money. At other times, we are not so practical. After all, you are talking about people who hold a three week carnival in the dead of winter each year. Only complete fools would do that!" he said.

CHAPTER SEVEN:
Legends and Other Lore

St. Augustine

They stood on the last remaining tower of Fort Matanzas. Harper pointed out to sea.

"The French came from that direction in two large galleons. They outnumbered the Spaniards by three to one. They would have taken St. Augustine easily as the Castillo had not yet been constructed. But Fate intervened. A great storm suddenly rose from the south. It roared up the coast and destroyed the galleons and killed many of the French soldiers.

The survivors, along with Ribault, staggered to shore. They came up right over there and were immediately confronted by Menendez and his men. Ribault tried to surrender. Menendez said he would allow them to surrender only under two conditions. They would have to swear allegiance to Spain and they would have to renounce their faith and become Catholics.

The French, who were Huguenots, refused to give up their religion. So Menendez ordered his men to kill every last one of them and throw their bodies into the sea. Some were shot. Most were hacked to pieces with swords. Just before he died, Ribault swore he'd return to kill Menendez and his soldiers no matter how long it took. Their bodies were loaded onto boats. The Spanish rowed them out to the deep water and threw them overboard.

It is said that each year on the anniversary of the massacre the sea around Matanzas turns blood red. I personally have never seen this happen but my father said he saw it when he was very young," he said.

"How many Huguenots were butchered?" asked Rick.

"Spanish records put the number at 270," Harper replied. "But their cruelties knew no bounds. They had already enslaved and massacred most of the natives in this region by then. My ancestors despised them. They worked our men and children to death and raped our women without fear of reprisals. The Church did nothing but look the other way. Hell, some of the priests also raped our women then had them excommunicated when they became pregnant. Those were very sad times for us. My ancestors should have killed Ponce de Leon When he came ashore. They never suspected the miseries he foretold."

"How are things now?" Rick asked.

"All of that happened over 2,000 years ago. That has little to do with us now, but we will never forget. If we do, it might happen again one day," Harper said.

They watched the sun sink in the west.

"I don't sail at night. We can build a fire from driftwood. I have some food in the cooler on board. It's safer to spend the night here," Harper said.

Midnight.

Rick and Mel stood outside the fort and watched the moonlight ripple across the waves. As they watched, they saw smaller lights in the water. They swirled around just below the surface. Rick shouted for Harper. The shaman woke up and hurried over and looked where Rick pointed.

"I have no idea what that is," Harper admitted.

The lights moved slowly toward the beach. Just as they reached the shore, they divided into two groups. One moved southward. The other headed straight toward the fort. Just as they reached the wall, they suddenly took on the shape of French colonial soldiers. The spirits looked up at them and charged. Mel r jumped down to confront them.

Rick and Harper watched as he positioned himself directly in front of the first spirit. The spirit stopped, glared at him, then charged. Mel opened up on him with both revolvers. The bullets passed straight through the phantom and struck the water a few yards offshore. The phantom seized him by the throat and pinned him against the wall.

Then he looked directly into his eyes and shook his head.

"Vous n'ete pas l'un d'eux," he said in a voice that seemed to come from miles away.

He released his grip and vanished.

Mel slumped to the ground and rubbed his throat. Rick and Harper hurried to him.

"What did he say?" asked Rick.

"It was in French but I think he said that I wasn't one of them," Mel said as Rick helped him to his feet.

Harper picked up Mel's hat and handed it to him.

"That makes perfect sense," Harper said. "If they are out to kill all of the descendants of the Spanish soldiers, then they have no beef with you."

"That still doesn't answer our questions," Rick said.

"Why in Hell did you shoot him? You can't kill someone who is already dead with bullets," Harper asked.

"Reflex action. I also needed to know if they were actually ghosts," Mel said.

"And are they?" Harper inquired.

"Hell yeah!" Mel answered.

Quebec

That night, they dined at the 1640 Restaurant in the hotel. The meal was more than excellent and they ordered drinks. Over dinner they discussed the situation.

Hunter sipped his Cognac.

"What eats dead bodies?" he asked.

"You mean besides the usual carrion eaters?" DuCassal asked.

"Yes. Rule out all of the natural ones. Think supernatural," Hunter said.

"Ghouls come to mind," DuCassal said. "They supposedly dine on freshly buried corpses."

"True. But they never eat long-dead, decayed corpses. They also shun all contact with the living. They never attack or kidnap adult humans. They have been known to kidnap human infants and substitute their own," Hunter said.

"Changelings," Lorena said. "The ghouls raise the humans as their own and they become just like them while the unsuspecting humans are stuck with a bizarre creature that detests light and cooked meats. It's a terribly unfair exchange."

"I'll say it is," DuCassal agreed.

"The things up here do eat the dead. They began by digging up and eating freshly buried bodies then resorted to eating the older corpses when the people started cremating their dead," Hunter pointed out.

"That still says ghouls to me, mon ami. Starving ones, but ghouls nonetheless," DuCassal said.

"Unless you factor in the kidnappings and attacks on the living," Hunter said.

"Ghouls would never do such things. Not even ghouls who were dying of hunger," Lorena said.

"Right. But if those things aren't ghouls, what in Heaven's name, are they?" Hunter asked.

Montcalm walked down the hill of Cote de Palais toward the ancient ramparts. He was going to check on his men before retiring to his quarters at the Citadel. This part of the ramparts overlooked Place de la Gare just to the east of Quartier St. Roch. Over the centuries, a forest had sprung up to the north of the old train station and it now extended all the way to the edge of the water at Port Samson.

And it was there that the loudest howls usually came from.

When he reached McMahon, he heard several shots ring out. He drew his sidearm and hurried his pace. When he reached the edge of the park behind the battlements, he heard more shots. Two of his men came running up to him. They stopped and saluted.

"Report!" Montcalm said.

"Several of those things have gotten inside the city. We are tracking them right now, Sir," one man said.

"Search everywhere. Don't miss anything and shoot to kill," Montcalm ordered.

The men saluted again and hurried off. Montcalm watched them leave then continued down McMahon. That's when he spotted something moving in the shadows between two buildings. He stopped and shouted at the figure.

It stopped and stepped into the light of the street lamp. Then it hissed and came at him. Montcalm raised his pistol and fired point-blank. The bullet entered the creature's forehead and exploded from the back of its skull, scattering bone, blood and bits of brain into the air. It staggered and fell face first in the snow. After a few twitches, it became very still.

Montcalm walked over and fired another shot into the back of its head. The creature twitched from the impact then went still.

Several of his men rushed up and saluted as he holstered his pistol.

"It's all clear, Sir," one reported. "We have found no other creatures."

"Are you absolutely certain?" Montcalm asked.

"Oui, mon colonel," the soldier replied. "The others have vanished. I do know that we managed to wound at least two others."

"Was anyone taken?" Montcalm asked.

"We won't know that until we check the area, Sir," the soldier said.

Montcalm pointed to the dead creature.

"Take this thing over to Dr. LeVant's office so he can examine it," he ordered.

Two of the picked up the creature and carried off down the street. Montcalm decided to return to the hotel and inform Hunter of the latest incident.

He found them still having dinner at the 1640.

He rushed up to their table and begged their pardon for interrupting their meal. Then he told them what had happened.

"How did they get in?" asked Hunter.

"No one knows for sure. Had they not been seen by two of the men, they might have been in and out of the city without anyone realizing it," Montcalm said.

"Any casualties?" Hunter asked.

"The only one I am aware of is the creature I killed," Montcalm said.

"Where is it now?" asked Lorena.

"I had my men take it to Dr. LeVant's house," Montcalm replied.

"Let's go and have a look at this thing," Hunter said as they walked out of the restaurant.

St. Augustine

The next morning, Rick, Mel and Harper walked over to the Government House to tell Lopez what happened. Lopez nodded.

"That clinches it. This definitely has everything to do with Ribault's curse. They're only after the descendants of the soldiers who were involved in the massacre," he said.

"So how many descendants of those original soldiers are still alive?" Mel asked.

"Besides me, there are eight," Lopez replied.

"Anyone directly related to Menendez?" Rick asked.

"Herman Menendez Vargas claims he is," Lopez said. "To be honest, no one's really sure. The original soldiers intermarried with local Natives and with other families that came later. Most married Americans after Florida became part of the United States. But although most can trace their lineage back to 1565, the Menendez line is kind of blurry."

"I see. It could be important. Ribault's ghost won't rest easy until he finds and kills the last male in the Menendez line. He may save him for last, so he can savor his revenge," Rick said.

Pino rushed into the office. He looked as pale as snow.

"What's wrong, Padre?" asked Lopez.

"This!" he replied as he handed him what appeared to be an ancient parchment. "This was nailed to the door of the Cathedral this morning. I don't know what it says. I think it's in French."

"It is," said Mel.

The parchment read: Nous allons reprendre la vie qui ont ete voles de nous.

"What it say?" Lopez asked.

"It says: 'We shall take back the lives that have been stolen from us'," Mel translated. "And it's dated two nights from now."

"What's so significant about the date?" Rick asked.

"That's the date the massacre took place," Harper said. "Two nights from now marks the 2,700th anniversary of the massacre."

He looked through the window toward the shore.

"Whatever happens will come from the sea," he said. "Somewhere out there are 270 restless and angry spirits. They want justice. They want payment for the lives that were taken from them."

"If I were Ribault, I'd carry out my original attack on the city. I'd try to burn it to the ground," Pino said.

Rick nodded.

"But I don't think that's what he wants," he said. "If I were descended from those Spanish soldiers, I'd be afraid. Very afraid."

"What's your plan?" asked Lopez.

"If I were you, I'd mobilize every man I could, arm them as best as I could and have them assemble on the beach near Matanzas," Rick said.

"Bullets won't stop those things. You said so yourself," Potter pointed out.

"True. But perhaps a show of force might cause them to back off," Rick said.

"It sure beats the Hell out of sitting around here and doing nothing," Potter said.

"I'll go with you," Harper said. 'There's an ancient Timucuan ceremony my ancestors have passed down to me. It's supposed to keep the dead at rest and provide protection for the living. I could give that a try."

"There's a lot of merit in ancient rituals. I've seen them work time and again. But they need to be performed exactly correct. One mispronounced word, wrong gesture or erroneous dance step or drum beat and it will fall to pieces," Rick agreed.

Harper smiled.

"I guess it can't hurt to try," he said.

"Do you think it'll work?" asked Lopez.

"Beats me, Tony. I've never tried it before," Harper said.

Rick and Mel looked at each other and laughed.

Quebec

Hunter stared at the body.

"What in God's name is that?" he asked.

"Be damned if I know, monsieur," LeVant said. "No one else knows, either. What they are and where they have come from remains a great mystery."

"You say you killed it with one shot?" Hunter asked.

Montcalm nodded.

"I was surprised it went down so easily. I thought these things would be harder to kill," he said.

"Loupgarou?" DuCassal asked.

Hunter shook his head.

"When you kill a werewolf, it reverts to its human form. This thing remained the same. Therefore, it can't possibly be a werewolf. Was there anything on him?" he asked.

LeVant reached into his pocket and pulled out a small gold locket on a chain.

"It had this around its neck," he explained.

"A locket. It's finely made, too. It has the initials RL etched into it," Hunter said as he examined it.

"Perhaps he took it from one of his victims?" suggested DuCassal.

Hunter shook his head.

"That's unlikely. I'd guess he was already wearing it when he became this thing," Hunter said. "A locket lie this is a very personal item. It's either a keepsake or memento. I can't imagine this thing killing someone then taking that person's locket and hanging it around his own neck."

"Neither can I, mon cher," Lorena said. "Such a thing would border on the absurd."

"So, if he was already wearing the locket—" DuCassal began.

"—He must have been human at one time," LeVant finished.

"Bingo!" Hunter smiled.

LeVant and Montcalm stared into space as they allowed the implication to sink in.

Hunter smiled at Marquand as he walked in and looked the creature over. The Governor-General shook his head.

"Now will you call up the reserves?" Montcalm asked.

"This is too close to home. We must at least double the number of men on active duty to keep them out of the city. I will call up the first 300 men on the roster tomorrow morning," Marquand replied.

"What about our friend here?" asked DuCassal.

"I think there's someone in this city who knows what this locket means. Perhaps someone who was very close to that thing. We need to find out who that person is," Hunter said.

They left LeVant's office and walked over to Place d'Arms. Hunter walked over to the stature of Champlain and placed the locket at his feet.

"Now all we have to do is wait and see who claims it," he said as they walked back toward the hotel.

"What if no one does, mon ami?" asked DuCassal.

"Someone will—after we tell Marquand to get the word out about it," Hunter assured him.

"But what if no one does, mon cher? How long will you wait?" Lorena asked.

"I'll wait a week. If no one claims the locket, I'll give it to Montcalm for a souvenir," Hunter smiled.

St. Francois.

Lauren Lamour was in her office, working late as usual. The sun had gone down hours before and she was growing tired. As she went over the latest budget report, a strange sucking sound, like water oozing down a drain, caught her attention. She looked up just in time to see a malformed humanoid creature slowly coming through her office wall.

She fought off an urge to flee. Instead, she reached for the loaded pistol she always kept in her desk drawer. The creature saw her and made a smacking sound with its twisted mouth as it moved toward her.

Lamour raised the pistol and fired.

The bullet entered the creature's face and erupted from the back of its skull and splattered the wall behind with a sickly pink liquid.

She walked over and put a second bullet into its chest as it lay twitching on the floor.

"Picked the wrong office, didn't you?" she said as she crouched next to it.

Her assistant, Bergere, heard the shots. He dropped his coffee mug and rushed into Lamour's office. He saw her kneeling next to the dead creature with a pistol in her right hand. She smiled at him.

"Are you alright, Lauren?" he asked as he crouched next to her.

"I'm in much better condition that my visitor," she said.

"What in God's name is that thing?" Bergere asked as he studied the hideous corpse.

"Beats me, Carl. Whatever it is, it can walk through solid walls," Lamour said.

"Maybe this is what has been eating the bodies?" Bergere suggested.

"Maybe. Have a couple of men come in and clean this place up tonight. First thing tomorrow, I want you to go to the redoubt and tell Pike what's happened. It's time to turn this over to the Guard," she ordered.

Quebec

Hunter watched as a tall woman dressed in a long, heavy overcoat walked up to the statue. From what he saw, her skin was pale, almost to the point of being colorless. Almost white, perhaps platinum locks peaked out from the folds on the sides of her hood.

She stopped and looked around for second or two as if fearful that someone might be watching. She stepped closer and visibly sighed as if the entire weight of the world was on her shoulders. She read the sign for few seconds then reached up and gingerly took the locket from its peg. She turned and almost jumped out of her coat when she saw Hunter standing behind her.

"Where'd you come from?" she asked after she caught her breath. "You scared the daylights out of me!"

"I was standing the shadows between the trees. I've been waiting for you," he said.

"For me?" she asked.

"For someone anyway," he said as he stepped closer. "Tell me about the locket."

She opened her hand and sighed. Tears formed in her eyes and rolled down her face.

"It was mine. He gave it to me as an anniversary gift three years ago. He said it would bring me good luck. When this trouble started, I placed it around his neck before he went to the Citadel for training. That was the last time I saw or spoke with him. I guess the locket didn't work," she said softly.

"He was your husband?" Hunter asked.

She nodded and sniffed.

"Oui. I wasn't sure until I saw the locket," she said.

"The initials?" he asked.

"Rowan Limy. That's my name," she replied. "Where did you find it?"

"It was around the neck of the creature Montcalm shot two nights ago," he said.

"Was it Andre? Was it my husband?" she asked tearfully.

"I really couldn't say," Hunter replied.

"Where is the body now?" she asked.

"Montcalm had it cremated. The ashes are in an urn at the church," Hunter said.

"Do you think I could claim them? I would like to give Andre a proper funeral," she said.

"I'm sure Father Challons will give them to you," Hunter said. "I'll walk over with you if you like."

"I would like that very much. What is your name, monsieur?" she asked as she dried her tears away on her sleeve.

"Hunter. Charles Hunter," he replied.

"I am pleased to meet you, Msr. Hunter," she said as she shook his hand.

"Just call me Hunter. Everyone else does," he said. "How old are you Rowan?"

"Seventeen. Andre and I had been married only one year. And now, it appears that I am a widow," she said sadly.

He walked her down the winding streets until they reached LeVant's office. She looked at Hunter. He nodded.

She knocked on the ancient wooden door. Seconds later, LeVant opened it. He scowled at her then let them in when he saw Hunter was with her.

"And what may I help you with on this cold evening?" he asked.

"I heard that Colonel Montcalm brought one of those creatures here and it was wearing this locket," Rowan said as she held the locket up.

"That is quite true, Madame. But why should that concern you?" LeVant asked.

"This is the locket I placed around the neck of my husband several weeks ago. I want to see the creature who wore it," she replied.

"Are you sure?" LeVant asked.

"Oui. I have to see the creature. I want to know if it might be my husband. Please, Doctor!" Rowan said.

"Alright. But I must warn you that it is not a pretty sight," LeVant said.

He led them to the back office. The body was on a long table and covered by a white sheet. LeVant walked over and pulled the sheet back to reveal the malformed face and twisted body. The moment Rowan saw the face, she swooned. Hunter caught her before she hit the floor and carried her into the outer parlor. He sat her up on the cou8ch and fanned her with his hat until she revived. Levant poured some brandy into a glass and handed it to her. Rowan pushed it away and shook her head. LeVant shrugged and drank it himself.

"I—I am alright now," she said. "I need to go back inside. I must see his face."

Hunter and LeVant escorted her back into the room. She walked to the table and uncovered the creature's face. They watched as she stared at it for a long time.

"Oui. That is him. That is my Andre," she said softly.

"Are you certain, Madame?" asked LeVant.

She nodded.

"It's the eyes. I'd know them anywhere. That is—or was—my husband," she replied.

"What would you have us do with his remains?" LeVant asked.

"Cremate him. I cannot bear the thought of those creatures eating him," she said.

"Good choice," Hunter said.

"Actually, you have no choice in the matter. You are aware of the Governor-General's edict, I am sure," LeVant said as they left the office.

Rowan nodded.

"The only way you could have claimed his body was if you could prove you had a crypt or vault to place him into," LeVant said. "All others must be cremated."

"We are both from families of very modest means, Doctor. Unfortunately, neither side has a crypt. Will I be allowed to keep his ashes?" she asked.

"His ashes are yours to do with as wish," LeVant assured her.

"Merci—both of you," she said.

Hunter watched her walk away and vanish around a corner.

"Poor thing. So sad to be widowed at such a young age," LeVant sighed as Hunter followed him back inside.

LeVant poured each of them a brandy.

"Have you ever seen her before?" Hunter asked as he sipped.

"I cannot say for sure," LeVant said. "Did you notice how sickly she looked? Almost anemic."

Hunter nodded.

"Could it be the plague you spoke of?" he asked.

"No. The victims do not turn so pale and they are totally incapacitated by the disease the moment it strikes. Perhaps she is just naturally so pale? You know, an albino?" LeVant suggested.

"I thought albinos normally had pink eyes," Hunter smiled.

"In the animal kingdom, that is true. Among humans, the eye colors vary. Hers are a very light blue," LeVant said. "In a strange way, she is very pretty, don't you think?"

"Yes. She does have a strange attraction to her," Hunter agreed. "At least we can put a name to that creature. Andre Limy."

"Limy? I know that family. They live in the St. Roche area," LeVant said. "They will be very saddened when they learn the fate of their son."

Since Andre Limy was now identified, Montcalm decided to give him a proper funeral at Notre-Dam with Father Challons presiding over the services. Two days later, Hunter, Lorena and DuCassal walked into the church. Challons, Marquand, Montcalm, LeVant and several uniformed soldiers were already in attendance. As soon as they saw Hunter, LeVant and Montcalm walked over.

"Did you notify the Lamy family?" Hunter asked.

"Oui. But Msr. Lamy informed me that do not have a son named Andre. In fact, he has no sons at all. Only three daughters he is trying to marry off," LeVant replied as they sat down in one of the pews.

"Then who's in that urn?" Hunter asked.

"According to his enlistment papers his name is Andre Lamy and that is all I know about him," Montcalm said.

"Nothing else?" Hunter asked.

"No. When a man joins the Guard, we don't inquire about his family background or personal history. We assume he is who he claims to be. As long as he can be trained and trusted to obey orders, we don't care about anything else," Montcalm explained.

"You make the Guard sound like the French Foreign Legion," DuCassal remarked.

"In many ways, it is," Montcalm said.

The door creaked open. They watched as Rowen entered. She was dressed in black and a veil covered her pale features. She walked down the aisle and took her place in the first pew.

"There's the grieving widow," Lorena said.

"If that's who she really is," Hunter said.

"They must have been in some sort of a relationship. Otherwise, she would not be here," Lorena said.

"True. But exactly what was their relationship?" Hunter wondered.

Father Challons walked to the front of the altar and said a prayer for the deceased. He kept it short and respectful. Montcalm stepped forward and commended the late Andre for his exemplary service to the Guard. When he was finished, he turned, snapped to attention, and saluted the urn. When he stepped aside, one by one, the other soldiers approached the urn and saluted. As they filed past Rowen, each of them handed her a single red rose. Hunter could see the tears rolling down her cheeks even under the veil.

The entire squad walked to the back of the church and stood at ease while Challons picked up the urn and handed it to Rowen.

"Merci, Pere," she said softly. "Merci."

She tucked the urn beneath the fold of her cloak and headed for the door.

Hunter waited until she left the church, then followed her at a safe distance. She walked north on Sainte Famille. Hunter followed a few yards behind, making sure to stay out of her line of sight. He just had to see what she was going to do with the ashes.

When they reached Mengerie, a heavy fog rolled in from the river. Even though it was quite thick, Hunter was able to keep sight of Rowen. When she reached Rue des Remparts, she turned left—and vanished.

An astonished Hunter spent the next several minutes searching for any sign of her. Realizing his efforts were futile, he gave up and walked back toward the hotel. He found DuCassal and Lorena seated inside the 1640 restaurant and joined them.

"So, where did she go?" asked DuCassal.

"I don't know," Hunter replied. "I lost her in the fog that rolled in from the river. I was still able to see her but after a while she just vanished."

"Vanished?" DuCassal asked.

"Yes. Like a ghost. One second she was right in front of me. The next, she was gone," Hunter said. "I looked around for a few minutes, then gave up."

"Interesting," DuCassal remarked.

"Very. There's something about her that bothers me, too. If she's not who she says she is, then why did she take those ashes? What does she want with them?" Hunter mused.

The next morning, they boarded the ferry with Montcalm and went across the river to Levis. When they slid up to the dock, they saw several fishermen working on their boats just as they did every spring. A few shouted greeting and waved. Montcalm waved and shouted back. The ferry captain blew the whistle to warn everyone aboard of the forthcoming jolt as the vessel bumped into the pier. As soon as it was in position, two of the crewmen jumped out and moored the craft to the two large posts, while two others lowered the gangplank.

As they stopped onto the dock, a large, bearded man walked up and shook hands with Montcalm.

"Long time, no see, Jack!" Montcalm said as they pounded each other on the back.

"It's good to see you, Yves! And the ferry. Now that it has made its first crossing, we know that winter is finally over. This one was far too long. And too damned cold," the man said. "I must make my boat ready now. Nice seeing you again."

He hurried over to one of the larger boats and jumped aboard. Montcalm led them up the main streets past one and two story red-roofed homes and shops, to a three story, dark stone building with a clock tower.

They walked inside and turned right until they reached a large, oak door with a glass pane. Montcalm knocked.

"Entre vouz!" a man shouted.

They walked in. Montcalm shook hands with Leonard Haynes, then made the introductions.

"What brings you here on this beautiful, sunny day?" Haynes asked.

"Have you had any strange occurrences over the winter?" Montcalm asked.

"Like what?" Haynes asked.

"Like disappearances, desecrated graves or anyone falling ill and dying from a strange malady?" Montcalm asked.

"No, Colonel. All is well here in Levis. The bitter cold and deep snows have kept the city shut down all winter, but with the thaw comes new life—as always. It's been a very good winter. In fact, no one has gotten or died or winter. Everyone here in Levis is doing just fine. Why do you ask?" Haynes answered.

Hunter told him what was going in Quebec.

Haynes whistled.

"That is indeed terrible. But I can assure you that no such things have happened here," he said. "No one has gone missing. No graves were dug up and no one has come down with that illness. But if any of those things do occur, I will inform you at once."

They took their leave and returned to Quebec.

Hunter looked up at the Citadel and wondered if the creatures would become bold enough to try to attack it. The ancient fortress looked impregnable from every angle. Its weakest side was the wall inside the city itself. In order to attack it there, they would first have to overrun Quebec.

"No," he thought. "They'd never attack the Citadel. They'd have to get at it another way."

Lorena smiled.

She could easily read his surface thoughts.

"Why did your ancestor march out to meet the British on the Plains?" she asked.

"We'll never know for sure, Madame," Montcalm replied. "Some have written that he did not trust the city's fortifications. He did not think the walls could withstand a direct assault. But as far as anyone knows, he never explained himself. Did he, Msr. Hunter?"

"No. He did not," Hunter said. "It's very sad, too. It was his lone mistake in an otherwise brilliant military career—and it cost France Quebec."

"But Wolfe didn't live to see the city surrender, either," Montcalm said. "Did you perchance have the opportunity to speak with my ancestor before he died?"

"Just for a second. He looked at me and said, 'You were right, Capitan,'. Then he lapsed into a coma," Hunter said. "It was a sad day for France. Your ancestor was my friend. A good friend. I missed him for quite some time afterward."

Montcalm nodded.

"You have given me some insight to his character I did not know about. For that, I thank you," he said.

"Tomorrow, we shall take the patrol boat upriver to Portneuf and the redoubt. We have not had contact with them since the first snowfall."

"And after that?" Hunter asked.

"We move on to Montreal," Montcalm replied.

CHAPTER EIGHT:
An Average Night on the Beach

St. Augustine

Midnight.

Potter arrayed his men in a single line just beyond the water's edge. There were 162 soldiers, armed with a wide variety of rifles and muskets. He had called up every last reserve officer he could find and had them don the official uniform of the St. Augustine Militia. The uniforms were almost exact copies of the ones originally worn by the Spanish soldiers in 1565.

Lopez and Harper were on the beach with them. Rick and Mel rode over to the ruined fort and climbed the tower so they could watch the water for any signs of unusual activity. The entire scene was brightly lit by the full moon above.

Harper, dressed in his full ceremonial costume and carrying a decorated lance, began his ritual at exactly midnight. He danced and chanted as he made intricate movements with the lance.

A few minutes into the ceremony, Mel pointed to a series of lights in the water. They were about 100 years offshore.

Rick nodded and shouted at Harper.

"Here they come!"

Then he and Mel raced down to the beach. They all stood and watched as three companies of very wet looking French soldiers marched out of the sea and moved inland. They stopped less than 50 feet from Potter's men.

It looked like a historical re-enactment as two early "colonial" armies faced each other. Potter's men in the copies of the early Spanish uniforms. Ribault's soldiers in the very same uniforms they had worn on the day they were massacred.

Potter and Lopez knew that any attempt to stop the French with bullets was futile. At best, they were putting on a display of force. All of their hopes now rested on Harper's ability to correctly perform the ancient ritual. If he was off by so much as a whisker, all would be lost.

The ghost of Ribault strode up to Harper who drew a line in the sand with his lance.

"Return to your resting place and leave the living in peace!" Harper commanded. "You cannot pass this line!"

Ribault grinned at him then erased the line with his boot. Harper held the lance in front of him with both hands. Ribault cut it in half with his saber. Then he pointed toward St. Augustine.

Rick and Mel reached Harper's side a second later. Mel shoved the shaman aside and stepped toward Ribault who eyed him with curiosity.

He smiled as Mel addressed him in French.

"Do I have the honor of addressing Msr. Ribault?" Mel asked.

"I am he," the spirit responded.

"Would you be so generous as to answer a question for me?" Mel asked.

"Ask," Ribault said.

"You have slumbered for 27 centuries. What has caused you to stir after all this time? What brings you here now?" Mel asked.

"We come because *he* has returned," Ribault said as he pointed his finger at Lopez. "Now the curse can be fulfilled."

"And who is he that causes you to act?" Mel asked.

"Menendez the Butcher," Ribault replied venomously. "No more talk!"

Before Mel could utter another word, Ribault turned and strode back to his waiting regiment. Rick and Mel hurried over to Lopez and told him what Ribault had said.

"You mean that I'm the cause of this?" Lopez asked in shock.

"What did he mean by you've returned?" asked Mel.

"I was born in Savannah. I came to St. Augustine to take the job as mayor. But that was several years ago. This doesn't make any sense!" Lopez said.

"Think—has anything happened lately that disturbed the waters around Fort Matanzas?" Rick asked.

"There was a terrible storm here about eight months ago. The storm destroyed much of the old fort and tossed debris up onto the beach for miles. Things that had been in the sea for centuries," Harper said.

"A hurricane?" Mel asked.

"No. This had too much lightning. The sea was lit up for miles in all directions as lightning struck the waves several times. One bolt actually hit the fort and blew it to pieces," Harper replied.

"That's it! The storm disturbed their resting place and the lightning supplied them with enough energy to carry out Ribault's curse!" Mel said.

"What do we do about it?" asked Lopez.

"I suggest that you order your men to retreat back into the city right now. Rifles and bullets are useless against those who are already dead," Rick said as a storm began to take shape miles out at sea.

The wind kicked up and roiled the waves. Seconds later, a heavy rain began to fall and lightning lit the sky.

'They're advancing!" Potter shouted. "Stand your ground, men!"

"No! Get out of here now! Get back to the Cathedral. They won't follow you inside," Mel shouted to deaf ears.

The French advanced until they were within 20 yards of Potter's men. Mel, Rick and Harper watched helplessly as both armies raised their rifles and fired. The rifle fire drowned out the thunder and filled the beach with dense smoke. When it cleared, all of the French soldiers were still standing and eight of the defenders, including Lopez, lay in pools of their own blood on the beach.

The French lowered their rifles and charged. Just before they struck Potter's line, they changed into bright balls of light and zipped toward the city.

"What just happened?" Potter asked.

"I think we lost," Rick said. "Let's get back to the city as quickly as possible."

Portneuf

It was early afternoon when the patrol boat bearing Montcalm, Hunter, Lorena and DuCassal and a squad of soldiers moored at the small dock at the base of the main road of Portneuf. The dock and village seemed eerily quiet as they followed the road into the heart of Portneuf. When they reached the village square, Montcalm began to feel uneasy.

There had been no signs of life so far.

No people.

No cats or dogs.

No birds.

No anything.

He turned to his men.

"Fan out and search for anyone who can tell us what happened here," he ordered.

They watched as the soldiers split into groups of threes and went down different streets. Then they continued across the square. When they came to the old church, Hunter stopped.

"If those things attacked, most people would flee to this church. It's a holy sanctuary against evil and as strong as a fortress," he said.

"Allo!" Montcalm shouted.

His voice echoed through the empty streets and faded away on the breeze.

Hunter knocked on the church's heavy doors. When no one answered, he pushed at them. They held fast.

"They're locked from inside," he said.

He stepped back and charged with his shoulder down. He hit the door so hard that the heavy brass bolt that had secured it came off and clattered against the stone floor inside. The doors swung inward.

"I smell blood. Human blood," Lorena said.

"How much?" Hunter asked as he drew his revolver.

"Enough to know that it came from several people," she replied as they entered.

The light streaming through the stained glass windows barely illuminated the inner sanctum and gave the place a sort of surrealistic atmosphere.

"I don't hear anything," she said. "The place is empty."

Hunter holstered his weapon and looked around. Bits of debris, like rifles and a few knives, broken rosaries and tiny crosses lay scattered amid the pews and along the aisles. Here and there, they saw dark brown-red splotches on the floor.

"There definitely was a struggle here," Hunter said. "Those things entered through the walls and attacked whoever was hiding inside."

"But where are they?" Montcalm asked.

Hunter smirked at him.

"Guess," he said.

When they walked back outside, they found the squad waiting for them in the square. Montcalm looked at the corporal.

"Report!" he ordered.

"We searched several streets and found no one. Portneuf has been abandoned, mon Colonel," the soldier replied.

"Let us head back to the boat and continue to the redoubt," Montcalm said.

They left Portneuf and sailed slowly up river until they came within sight of the ancient redoubt.

The bright red roofs of the redoubt's buildings glistened in the afternoon sun as they pulled into the small dock. Two small, ferry-like vessels were still moored to the pier. Other than the gulls crying and circling overhead, there were no other sounds or signs of life.

As they disembarked, Montcalm looked up the guard tower.

"That's odd. There should be a sentry on duty in the tower, but there is no one there now. If I find that he's been screwing off somewhere, I'll crucify him!" he said as they walked through the open gate.

"The tower and the dock aren't the only places that are deserted," Lorena said. "I sense no movement of any kind inside."

They pulled into the dock. The gate was wide open. Montcalm cursed at the inefficiency as they disembarked and entered the redoubt. The open area was littered with broken weapons and other discarded equipment. Here and there, they saw splotches of red mixed in with the snow.

Montcalm shouted.

His voice echoed through the redoubt eerily.

"I don't like the looks of this," Hunter said.

"Me neither, mom ami," DuCassal said as he checked the load in his shotgun. "I smell a trap."

They walked over to the barracks. The door was locked from inside. Hunter stepped back and kicked it open.

When they stepped inside, Montcalm turned on the lights. What they saw stunned them.

One man was lying face-down in the middle of the room with his back torn open and a pistol in his right hand. A dried blood stain spread out beneath him. Another sat propped up against the wall with his face chewed off. He also looked as if he'd been eviscerated. His blood was also everywhere.

Three other men were in the next room, also in various degrees of dismemberment and they, too, looked as if they'd had chunks of flesh bitten from them. Spent cartridges were scattered all over the floor, but there were no signs of any dead creatures.

"At least they went down swinging," DuCassal said.

The rest of the barracks were empty.

They walked over to the mess hall. Inside, they found tables and chairs overturned and dishes and utensils lay everywhere. Among the debris they found two more soldiers. Most of their flesh had been stripped from them and parts of their bodies lay in several places.

They walked to the kitchen and found the cook lying on his back with a meat cleaver in his right hand. His throat had been chewed out and his chest ripped apart to expose the ribs. His internal organs were missing.

"Those things must have come through the walls and caught them by surprise," Lorena said. "They never knew what hit them."

Montcalm was nearly in tears at what he saw. Portneuf was lost. And his men had paid a terrible price trying to defend it.

They walked outside. The sun was beginning to set in the west and its rays were turning the sky from deep blue to golden orange.

"This has become my worst nightmare," Montcalm said. "How do we fight creatures like this?"

"I wonder if the plague also reached this place," DuCassal said.

"There's one way to check," Hunter said as he looked at Montcalm. "Do they have a cemetery here?"

"Oui. There is a small one behind the chapel," Montcalm replied.

"Take us there," Hunter said.

The cemetery was a wreck. The small patch of ground next to the chapel contained 34 graves, most of which were several years old. These were still undisturbed and their inhabitants slept quietly beneath the snow blanketed earth.

But several other graves told a starkly different tale. They found that all of the newer graves had been dug up and the caskets broken into. They also found that all of the corpses had been eaten and their bones tossed aside like so much trash.

Montcalm made the sign of the cross and shook his head.

"Looks like the plague also reached this redoubt," Hunter said.

"We had no way of knowing this until now," Montcalm said sadly.

"And those things showed up to fed upon the dead, just as they did in Quebec and the village," Lorena said as she looked around. "These things are clever, Hunter. They don't leave any kind of trail that I can follow."

"You said you had 100 men here," Hunter said. "There are 34 graves here and we counted 17 more in other parts of the redoubt. That makes 51. There are 49 others unaccounted for. Where are they?"

"Perhaps those things took them?" Ducassal suggested.

"Or maybe they abandoned the post and fled to Montreal?" Hunter added. "That's what I'd do in their situation."

"Impossible! These are the finest and bravest soldiers in all of Canada. They would never leave their post under any circumstances. They would stay and defend it to the last man," Montcalm insisted.

Hunter looked at him.

"If that's true, then where are their bodies? They should by lying all over the place, yet there's no sign of them anywhere. It seems we have a real mystery on our hands now, Colonel," he said.

"I am as perplexed as you are, Msr. Hunter," Montcalm said as they looked around.

"Your men were faced with extraordinary conditions and circumstances. Any sane person, no matter how well trained or courageous, would have retreated to safer place. I feel that your men escaped to Montreal," DuCassal said.

"I hope you are right, Monsieur," Montcalm said.

"There's one sure way to find out," Hunter said. "Let's head to Montreal. Before we go, Let's make sure we didn't miss anyone."

"There are another row of barracks across the compound," Montcalm said.

They walked across the open parade ground and headed for another long, stone, two story building that looked much like all of the other structures in the redoubt. The doors were all closed and the windows were shuttered. Hunter walked to the first door and pushed.

"It's locked from the inside," he said as he stepped back and kicked it open.

Almost immediately, the stench of rotting flesh caught their attention. They stepped inside and saw nothing but pools of dark, dried blood on the floor and similar splatters on the walls. The furniture was strewn all over the open bay and spent cartridges, belts, bits of uniforms and a couple of rifles lay scattered on the floor.

But there were no signs of any bodies.

Anywhere.

"But I can smell it," Lorena said. "There has to be a body here somewhere."

DuCassal walked over to an overturned bunk and pulled away the mattresses and bed covers to reveal a half eaten corpse. He turned away to vomit.

"Looks like Jean-Paul found it," Hunter joked.

"This must have been one Hell of a fight," Montcalm said.

"They made a stand. Too bad it was their last stand," Hunter said as they left the barracks.

When they stepped outside, Hunter sensed something lurking on the roof. He stopped and drew his revolver just as the creature launched itself at him. Hunter ducked and rolled out of the way. The creature hit the ground, rolled and bounced back to its feet.

It hissed and came at him, claws outstretched and teeth bared.

Hunter fired twice.

The first bullet struck it in the chest and sent it reeling back a few feet. The second shot struck it in the center of its face and blew out the back of its skull. It spun a few times, gurgled horribly, and fell still.

Hunter holstered his weapon and watched as a pool of sickly pink spread out from beneath the creature and stained the snow. The others hurried over.

"That's one less to worry about," Hunter said. "Looks like he's wearing military trousers."

"Mon Dieu! Those are indeed regimental trousers. Could this creature have been one of my men?" Montcalm asked.

"He is not changing back into his human form," Lorena observed. "He cannot be a werewolf of any kind."

"No. He's not a werewolf. Neither was the one back in Quebec," Hunter said as he squatted down to examine the creature. "In fact, I've never seen anything like these creatures before."

"Nor have I, Charles," DuCassal said.

"If they are not loupgarou, then what in Heaven's name are they?" Montcalm asked,

"To be honest, I haven't a clue," Hunter said as he stood and looked around. "And I doubt that Heaven has anything at all to do with them."

"At least they can be killed. They are not invulnerable," Montcalm said.

"And now we have a fairly good idea of what happens to the people they take," Hunter said as they walked back toward the chapel.

"You think they take them so they can change them into other creatures? Why?" Montcalm asked.

"Perhaps to ensure the survival of their species. Or maybe they're trying to create enough of their kind to overrun all of Quebec," Hunter guessed. "Or perhaps there are other reasons we can't even guess at. Whatever it is, it doesn't bode well for the home team."

Montcalm looked around at the deserted redoubt.

"This has become the greatest tragedy in the entire history of the regiment," he said.

"Let's gather up all of the bodies and burn them," Hunter said.

"Good idea. It is much better than leaving them for those things to feed upon. At least we can deprive them of one source of nourishment," Montcalm agreed.

An hour later, the half frozen bodies of the slain soldiers were burning brightly in the middle of the parade field. As the thick, black smoke rose into the night air, the shadows beyond the redoubt became filled with angry howls . . .

CHAPTER NINE:
If it howls Like Werewolf

They reached Montreal two hours later. Much to their surprise, they found the port and most of the lower city well patrolled by Gaude's men. One of the recognized Montcalm when he stepped off the boat. He ran over and saluted.

Montcalm returned it.

"Take us to Chief Gaude," Montcalm said.

The soldier led them to the city hall and into Gaude's office, where he was conferring with Bourgue. They rose to shake hands as Montcalm made the introductions. Gaude looked at Hunter.

"I have heard of you—all of you," he said. "You have no idea how glad I am to see you."

"That's never a good sign," DuCassal said as they sat down.

"Tell us what's been happening here," Hunter said.

Gaude told them about the desecrated graves and the winter-long epidemic that had claimed more than 90 lives and how their bodies had been dug up and eaten within days of burial.

"We never saw what was doing it until two nights ago," he said. "Around midnight, these terrifying howls filled the air. They seemed to come from everywhere. The howls grew louder by the minute. At two a.m., one of my patrols encountered a group of the strangest creatures running along the pier and gave chase. They managed to shoot one but the rest just vanished into the shadows. We took the creature to the hospital and placed it into a drawer in the morgue for future study," he said.

"I'd like to see it," Hunter said.

"No problem. The hospital is just on the next street. We can go there now," Gaude said.

He led them two blocks down and into a large, well-maintained hospital. They walked past the emergency room and headed down the back steps to the morgue. The attendant let them and walked them to the drawer. Then he slid it open to reveal a sheeted figure.

Hunter pulled back the sheet.

"It's the same type of creature you killed in Quebec," he said to Montcalm.

"We feel it is some type of loupgarou," Gaude said.

"There's one problem with that and it's a large one," Hunter said.

"Eh?" Bourgue asked.

"Werewolves do not eat corpses. They only feed on fresh, living people. They're not carrion eaters. They're hunters," Hunter replied.

"But this creature resembles a loupgarou," Bourgue said.

"And they act and sound like loupgarous," Gaude added.

Hunter nodded.

"Usually, if it looks, acts and sounds like a werewolf, it is a werewolf. But not in this case," he said as he looked at the creature. "If it were, it would have reverted to its human form when you killed it. This stayed the same."

"But there is yet another piece of this puzzle, mes amis," DuCassal said.

"The virus. What is it? Where did it come from? What connection does it have to these creatures if any?" Hunter said as he paced.

He stopped and looked at Gaude.

"First, the virus showed up and killed dozens of people in Quebec. Then these creatures came from nowhere to feed on the fresh corpses. They also attack and kidnap living people and, when deprived of fresh corpses, they will dig up and eat long dead ones," he summarized. "Is that what's happening here?"

"Oui," Gaude said. "You have described our problems perfectly."

"We have also heard rumors that anyone who is bitten or scratched by the creatures changes into one but we have not been able to substantiate that," Montcalm said.

"We can," Gaude said. "Several of your men are in our dispensary. They are undergoing the transformation even as we speak."

"My soldiers are here?" Montcalm asked.

"Oui. Twenty three of them arrived just two days ago from Portneuf. Four were wounded and they all looked as if they'd been put Hell itself," Gaude said. "They were a most pitiful looking lot."

"I must speak with their commanding officer, Capt. Roche," Montcalm said.

"That will not be possible, Colonel," Brande said as he walked into the room.

"And why not?" Montcalm asked.

"Captain Roche sustained a minor wound in a skirmish against those things a few days ago. Within hours, he began to transform into one of them. As per his orders, I confined him and four other men to cells in our dungeon and assumed command of the redoubt. The next day, all of them had vanished into thin air," Brande said.

"You mean they escaped?" Montcalm asked.

"Oui. And their cells were locked from the outside and the bars on their windows were undisturbed. They simply disappeared without any trace," Brande said.

"Incredible! That means those things can walk through solid walls," Gaude said.

"This just keeps getting worse, mon ami," DuCassal said.

"What happened at the redoubt?" asked Hunter.

Brande shook his head.

"It was a nightmare. Those things attacked the village and we had to evacuate everyone we could to Montreal. Roche sent the villagers here on the flatboats along with half our men. The next night, they attacked the village again, as some of the people decided to stay and fight. When we reached it, those things were everywhere. They attacked us from all sides. The battle lasted three hours. When the sun rose, the creatures vanished," he said.

"We lost six men that night and 11 were wounded. The villagers lost double that number and the mayor told me that at least 20 were missing," he added.

He paused to collect his thoughts.

"The next night, they struck again. There was a blizzard that day and the road to the village was nearly impassable. It took us over an hour to reach it. When we did, dozens of those things were there. They were eating the bodies in the streets. I formed my men into squads and we made a sweep of the village. We shot and killed at least 30 of those things, but they rallied and counter attacked. When they vanished again at sunrise, bodies lay everywhere and at least four of the buildings were burning out of control," he said.

"Why didn't the villagers lock themselves indoors after the storm?" asked Montcalm.

"They did," Brande said. "According to the handful of survivors, those things came right through the walls after them. To avoid getting killed, they fled into the streets where more of the creatures were waiting."

"That sounds like a well coordinated attack," Hunter said. "That means that they're either intelligent enough to plan or someone's leading them."

Montcalm shuddered at the though.

"They took another 23 villagers that night and killed at least 30 more. The mayor, Pierre LeGrand, ordered all of the wounded to be locked up in the city jail. Then he and the surviving villagers moved into the church and fortified it. I don't know if it did them any good."

"It didn't," Montcalm said. "When we went to the village, we checked the church. It was locked from the inside. When we forced the doors open, the church was deserted."

"How did you end up here?" Hunter asked.

"After the last skirmish, ten of my men came down with and died from the plague. I could not bear the thought of those things eating them, so I had them cremated. I was down to 35 men. That was barely enough to defend the redoubt," Brande said.

"Those things must have known how weak we were because the following night, they attacked the redoubt. They also attacked the next two nights. After three such skirmishes, I made the decision to abandon the redoubt. Our situation had become untenable at best. While we were preparing to leave, those things attacked again. We barely managed to reach the longboats. That was just two nights ago," he added.

Montcalm looked at him.

"You did well, Lieutenant," he said. "Did they attack the village on those nights as well?"

"Truthfully, I do not know. The village was the furthest thing from my mind. I did not hear the alarm so I did not concern myself with it."

"Under the circumstances, you made the only possible decision. Had you not abandoned the redoubt, your entire company would have been wiped out," Montcalm assured him.

"Merci, Colonel. But your words do little to console me," Brande replied.

"Have you heard from the men at Fort Stewart?" Montcalm asked.

"No. But we can see the lights from the ramparts each night, so perhaps all is well," Bourgue said.

"The ice has on the river has broken up. We should be able to get to the fort tomorrow morning," Hunter suggested. "How many men are garrisoned there right now?"

"Fifty," Montcalm said. "It doubles during the warmer months. It's a small post and very quiet. We station our newer, less experienced soldiers there. Some of the men complain that the place is very dull."

"Let's hope it's stayed that way so far," Hunter said.

Brande looked down at the ground.

"What shall I do about our wounded?" he asked.

"I strongly recommend that you put a bullet through each of their skulls before their transformation is completed," Montcalm said. "I know that is a most difficult decision for you to make, but there is no other way. Those men are lost to us now anyway. It is better for them to die than to join those things out there."

Brande nodded.

"That's what Capt. Roche ordered me to do with him. Unfortunately, I never got the chance," he said.

"Do not let that happen again, Lieutenant," Montcalm said. "For their sakes."

"How many of your people have gone missing?" asked Hunter as they walked to Gaude's office.

"Fifty-seven at the last count," Gaude replied. "Seventeen were taken while they were in the UPN."

"What's the UPN?" asked Hunter.

"It's the Underground Pedestrian Network. It was constructed during the 20th century of the First Age as an underground entertainment and shopping network. There were over 1,700 shops and 200 restaurants down there as well as several theaters and night clubs. People could reach it from more than a dozen places and a few hotels. It was very popular during the winter months," Bourgue said. "We shut it down after those people went missing. All of the surface entries have been sealed."

"How large is it?" Hunter asked.

"It is 33 kilometers in total," Bourgue replied.

"That sounds a perfect lair for our friends," DuCassal remarked. "They love to live underground."

"Did you kill all of the lights when you sealed it?" Hunter asked.

"Oui. Why? Is that a bad idea?" Gaude asked.

"It might be. The darkness enables them to hide and multiply. Gates and sealed doors won't stop them, either. Eventually, they'll start prowling the city streets at night. They'll avoid the street lights and stick to the dark, unlit areas," Hunter said.

"There is enough space down there to conceal an entire army!" Gaude said.

"Right now, there's probably an entire nest of those things just waiting for the right moment to attack," Hunter said.

"If so, then we should launch a pre-emptive attack," Montcalm suggested.

"Oui. We could send our men in from several directions to cut off their escape. If we move quickly and with great stealth, we should be able to hunt them down and kill them before they realize what is happening," Gaude agreed.

Hunter scowled but said nothing. Both Lorena and DuCassal wanted to comment, but Hunter shook his head. Montcalm saw the look of disapproval on his face.

"You were a soldier. What would you suggest?" he asked.

"Before I say anything, I want to look at a map of the entire complex," Hunter said. "A good commander studies the terrain before invading it."

Montcalm laughed.

"I have several maps of the network in my office," Bourgue said. "The most recent was made 15 years ago when we added new lights to the darker areas."

They hurried over to City Hall. Bourgue walked to map cabinet and pulled a wide sheet of paper from which he proceeded to spread out across his desk.

"This was a very clever and ambitious project for its time," he said. "Winters here can be cruel but we here in Montreal love our night life, so we created this network to enable businesses to stay open and people to enjoy their normal routines without having to worry about the weather. Over time, it also became a major tourist attraction."

"Where do you enter it from?" asked Hunter.

"There are four main entrances," Gaude explained as he pointed tem out. "There are also a half dozen smaller ones. The rest were sealed decades ago for lack of use. Each of the main entrances leads into one of the larger areas of shops, restaurants, museum basements, galleries, hotels—you name it. In all, the UPN covers 33 kilometers interconnected by long tunnels and old subway lines."

Hunter studied the map for a few minutes, then turned to them.

"Here's my plan," Hunter began. "Arm every man you have with the heaviest caliber weapons available and divide them into ten groups. Four groups will enter the complex from a different place and move through it until they converge here at Place d'Armes. Along the way, have your men shoot anything they see. Above all, they are to avoid any hand-to-hand combat with those things. Have them move at a slow, steady pace and watch their backs at all times."

"I want every third man to carry a flashlight or lantern to illuminate any dark spaces those things might lurk in," he added. "The other six groups will guard the other entry points to prevent any escapes. Don't let any of those things get into the city."

He turned to the mayor.

"Do the lights still work?" he asked.

"Oui. They were all in excellent working order a few weeks ago," he said.

"How easily can they be turned on again?" Hunter asked.

"Very easily. The master switch is in Chief Gaude's office," Bourgue replied.

"Good. We'll move in at daybreak. At exactly eight a.m., I want you to turn on those lights. If I'm right, the lights will render those things nearly blind and give us the advantage," Hunter said.

"What if you're wrong, Msr. Hunter?" Gaude asked.

"In that case, be prepared for a long, hard battle," Hunter said.

"What do you hope to accomplish with this raid?" Montcalm asked.

"Two things, Colonel. First, I want to wipe out every single one of those things or at least drive them out of Montreal. Second, if we're really lucky, we may be able to find the place they entered from and follow it back to their main lair," Hunter replied.

"Sounds good to me. What time do you wish to launch the attack?" asked Montcalm.

"At sunrise tomorrow," Hunter said. "When those things are at their weakest."

Fort Stewart.

Lt. Passant stepped out into the morning cold. As he did, he coughed several times, then spat up a mass of yellow-green phlegm. He was starting to feel a little stronger. The cold or whatever it was, has lingered for several weeks and had made his life miserable.

Dr. Abraham and Sgt. LaMont greeted him.

Passant smiled and returned it. He looked up at the sky. The deep blue had finally replaced the cold, gray shroud that had hovered over the region all winter.

"How are the men?" he asked.

"So far, so good. None of them show any sign of the virus. I've heard that it has hit Montreal pretty hard and taken the lives of dozens of people there. We've been quite fortunate," Abraham said with a smile. "We've had just one death."

"Was it the virus?" Passant asked as they walked to the mess hall.

"No one seems to know what it was," LaMont replied. "But something very strange happened a few days after he was buried."

"What?" asked Passant.

"Something dug him up, broke into his casket and ate part of his corpse," Abraham said.

"That is strange. Was it an animal of some kind?" Passant asked as they entered the warm building and hung their coats up on one of the wooden pegs in the wall.

"If it was, it must have been starving. Animals normally don't dig up and eat dead bodies unless they are dying from hunger," LaMont said as he picked up one of the heavy steel trays and a cup from the rack at the end of the serving line.

"There was something else," Abraham said. "Two people have gone missing in the past few days. They were both on their way home from work. Neither of them ever made it. The locals searched for days but never found a trace of them."

They received their meals from the servers and sat down at a nearby table. Passant sipped his coffee. The disappearances bothered him.

"How long ago did they go missing?" he asked.

"The first went missing eight days ago. The second, three days ago," LaMont answered. "I've only found out about them this morning from Dr. Abraham."

Passant eyed Abraham.

"And why did you not tell me of this earlier?" he asked.

"I did not tell you because Msr. Duvall, the mayor, I wanted to handle it himself," Abraham said. "He said it was a civil matter."

Passant shook his head.

"Keep me informed of such things from now on, Doctor. I don't like surprises," he said.

Montreal.

Sunrise.

Hunter and Lorena walked over to the McGill entry where 24 soldiers waited. They were armed with rifles and pistols and each had an extra bandolier of bullets crossing his body. Several had lanterns and flashlights. A tall, bearded sergeant nodded and brought the squads to attention.

"We are ready, Msr. Hunter," he said.

Hunter looked up at the sky.

"Let's go," he said as two of the men opened the doors.

They walked down the flights of stairs to and stopped when they reached the bottom. The UPN reeked of urine and feces and rotting flesh. Several of the men rubbed their noses. Some tied kerchiefs around their faces which covered their mouths and noses. They waited. One by one, the banks of bright lights flickered to life to illuminate the entire network. Almost as soon as the lights came on, the tunnels became filled with yowls and screams of creatures in great pain and panic.

Hunter drew his revolvers and signaled the men to follow. They made their way down one of the main streets past underground entries to the hotels and museums above, long abandoned shops and restaurants and dusty kiosks. Most of the stores were also lit and the screams became louder and louder as they moved down the street.

As they neared a cross section, three of the creatures stumbled toward them, screaming and writhing in agony as blood dropped from their now ruptured eyes. Hunter shot all three down and watched them fall.

"Why do they bleed?" one soldier asked as he looked at the corpses.

"The lights. The glare destroys their optic nerves," Hunter explained as he stepped over them.

They soon encountered another creature. This one was kneeling on the floor clutching its face and wailing. The soldier next to Hunter raised his rifle and shot it through the head, putting it out of its misery. The creature pitched forward and lay still as they filed past.

While the main arteries were brightly lit, some of the shops and side tunnels had remained dark. Whenever they came to one of these areas, the men first shined their lights inside to flush the creatures out. At one such place, the lights angered a group of the things who had hidden themselves. Some of the creatures shrank away from the lights while others screamed and charged, only to be gunned down in short order. Some of them men went down the tunnel and finished off the remaining creatures.

Another groups charged out of a dark store only to be brought to their knees by the lanterns. While they screamed and clawed at their melting eyeballs, the soldiers finished them off and kept moving.

"They don't put up much of a fight," the sergeant observed.

"You wouldn't, either if your eyes were melting," Lorena said.

He laughed.

"You are right, of course," he said as he shot yet another creature through the face.

They walked on at a steady pace, searching out and killing creature after creature. Wounded and terrified, the creatures were easy targets for the trained soldiers. Almost none attacked. Most were either writhing in agony on the floor or vainly seeking out the darker places of the network.

DuCassal's group met with similar success.

They entered the UPN via the Place D'Arts and steadily moved toward the convention center. They killed creature after creature until they came to a long, dark corridor. DuCassal held up a fist then signaled for the men with the lanterns to move in ahead of the group. As soon as their light penetrated the tunnel, a score of angry creatures charges at them. The soldiers aimed the lights at the faces. The creatures stopped, covered their eyes, and retreated. DuCassal and the soldiers chased after them until they cornered them where the tunnel dead-ended. They were already bleeding from their eye sockets and screaming in pain. DuCassal stepped aside and allowed the soldiers to finish them.

He looked around as he reloaded his shotgun.

"It looks as if we have killed all of them," he stated. "Let's continue our stroll and see what else we can stir up."

The corridors ahead were filled with wails and screams of the stricken creatures who now fumbled around blindly. The soldiers shot every one they saw and even chased several down dark passages until they trapped and killed them, too.

DuCassal realized how helpless the creatures were in the bright lights. Without the use of their sight, they were like the proverbial sitting ducks and provided little more than target practice for him and the soldiers. DuCassal likened it to a "good old fashioned turkey shoot". Most of the creatures never knew what hit them or who fired the fatal shots.

DuCassal brought down two more creatures with the last of his shotgun shells. He slipped the weapon under his arm and drew his revolver.

Not a bad day's work. Twenty four shots. Twenty four kills. A perfect score," he said with a grin.

The men laughed.

"This is not a battle, Msr. DuCassal," one man said. "It is a slaughter."

"Good thing, too. If one of these things bites you, you'll become just like them in a few days," another man warned.

"I would not wish such a fate on anyone. Not even my mother-in-law," the first soldier said.

"I thought you said she was a beast," another man said.

"Oui. She is indeed a beast, but these things are much uglier," the soldier replied with a chuckle

The battle went pretty much the same for the other groups. The lights had disabled the creatures so badly they posed almost no threat at all. The soldiers made easy work of them as they made their sweep through the UPN.

The few creatures that attempted to flee from the UPN were quickly turned into pools of fetid, bubbly muck by the warm sunlight.

After eight hours, all of the groups met in the big open area of Place D'Armes. Gaude and Montcalm smiled when they saw the others. Hunter nodded.

After taking a head count to ensure that everyone was safe, they marched up the steps to the surface where the mayor and several soldiers waited. The sun was already setting in the west.

"How did it go?" Bourgue asked.

"Much easier than I anticipated," Gaude replied.

"It really wasn't much of a battle. Most of the creatures were blinded by the lights and were easy targets. The few who were not blinded, we hunted down and killed."

"Any casualties?" Bourgue asked.

"Not a one. No one got so much as a scratch," Montcalm replied.

"So your theory was right after all, Msr. Hunter. They cannot function in the bright lights or sunlight," Bourgue said as the soldiers filed past and headed back to their barracks.

"We were lucky. The lights dissolved their eyeballs and rendered them helpless. All we did was put them out of their misery. We swept the entire UPN. I think we killed hundreds of them," Hunter said as they walked toward City Hall.

"At least. I know that we ran out of ammunition," DuCassal smiled.

"So did we," Montcalm added.

"I highly recommend that you keep the lights on down there at least until this is over. You don't want them to try to colonize it again," Hunter said.

"So Montreal is now safe?" Bourgue asked.

"For now. There's no telling just how many of those things exist. Don't relax your guard. In fact, you should keep patrolling the UPN to make sure it stays safe," Hunter said.

"I think you should send some crews down there to gather up and burn the corpses. Do it outside the walls so their friends can see it. It will make for good shock value," DuCassal suggested.

Bourgue nodded.

"We shall cross to Ft. Stewart tomorrow," Montcalm said. "Tonight, we eat and rest."

Hunter looked at Lorena.

"You alright?" he asked.

"I'm fine, mon cher," she assured him. "But the time is getting close."

"You can use me if you have to," he offered.

"Merci, mon cher. I don't think it will come to that," Lorena smiled. "I don't want to risk returning you to your old habits."

He laughed, but he still felt worried. He was always amazed at how long she was able to go between feedings. He'd seen her go as long as a month without succumbing to the urge. But those last few days were always difficult for her.

"Do you have any dangerous criminals you need dealt with?" he asked.

"Not really. Our crimes are usually petty. Some thefts occur once in a while. Perhaps a brawl or two. But nothing of any urgency," Gaude said.

Hunter looked at Lorena.

She smiled weakly.

Fort Stewart

The next morning, they took the ferry to Fort Stewart. When they disembarked, Sgt. LaMont greeted them.

"It is good to see you again, Colonel," he said with a salute. "It has been a long and most unusual winter for us here."

"How so?" Montcalm inquired.

"I think it best that you receive that report from Lt. Passant, Sir," LaMont replied as he led them to the headquarters building.

Passant snapped to attention when they walked in.

"Be seated, Lieutenant," Montcalm said.

He made the introductions. They listened as Passant told them of the strange events that occurred around the fort.

Hunter looked at him.

"This means those creatures have made it over here," he said. "They haven't been active because they haven't had any fresh corpses to feed on."

"There can't be very many of them," DuCassal said. "None of the older graves have been disturbed and only two people have been taken. That tells me there's a small number of those things here."

"What things?" asked Passant.

Montcalm explained what had happened in other places. When he was finished, Passant looked at him like he'd gone insane. Montcalm saw the expression on his face and laughed.

"I can assure you that I have not lost my mind, Lt. Passant," he said. "It is all very real. Horrifyingly real."

"And you think this may happen here?" Passant asked.

"It will happen here unless we can locate their nest and exterminate them," Hunter said. "From what we've seen so far, these things probably dwell underground in old caves or tunnels. Are there any such places nearby?"

Passant thought for a moment and nodded.

"There is a sewer line that lies directly beneath the village. It was built centuries ago. Parts of it are still in use. Some are not and have been sealed off. It covers about 75 kilometers altogether," he said. "It includes a connection to the fort."

"Are there maps?" Hunter asked.

"I am sure they have some at the town hall," Passant replied. "We can ask Msr. Valons. He's the records keeper."

"Let's go," Hunter said.

Martin Valons was 85 years old and had snow white hair. He sported a handlebar mustache and wore pince nez glasses and he knew every inch of the local sewer tunnels.

Passant made the introductions. After everyone shook hands, Passant told them what they needed. Valons nodded.

He went into a back office and emerged bearing three large cardboard tubes. He uncapped each and pulled out the ancient diagrams and gently rolled them out on the table.

"The sewers were constructed between 1854 and 1888 of the First Age," he said. "The main lines were done first then connections to each structure were added as the city grew. As the city retracted, the smaller lines were disconnected and sealed up with bricks. Now, the only lines in use are the two main lines."

As he talked he ran his fingers over the blueprints to show what he was talking about.

"Where do the main lines empty into the river?" Hunter asked.

Valons pointed to two places. One led directly from the town to the river. Another led from the fort to the river. He pointed to several other lines.

"These are run-offs. When the snow melts, the water drains into them and flows into the river. The sewage waste goes through a double purification system before reaching the river so as not to contaminate the fishing grounds," he explained.

"Are these usually filled with water?" Hunter asked.

"Oui," Valons said. "The water in them is usually neck deep."

DuCassal nodded.

"I think we can safely rule out the main lines and drains," he said.

"What about the older lines? Would they be large enough for something to live in?" Hunter asked.

Valons saw he was serious. He pointed to two places.

"Both of these lines once led into large storage areas beneath the city. Water was diverted to each of these places and held there so as not to put too much strain on the main lines during the thawing seasons. Each place is more than large enough for someone to hide in," he said.

"Then that's where we'll start," Hunter said.

"Agreed," Montcalm nodded. "How would one access those areas?"

"There are four maintenance entries in the city and two just outside in these woods," Valons said as he showed them on the plans. "Only two maintenance entries are still in use and both entries in the woods were sealed at least 100 years ago."

"Which leads to what area?" asked Montcalm.

"They are interconnected. You can reach both holding areas from any entry. Once you reach the main tunnel, it's easy," Valons said.

"Merci, Msr. Valons. You have been a great help," Montcalm said as they all shook hands.

Passant sneezed as they left the office.

"When do you want to do this?" he asked.

"As soon as we come up with a plan of operation," Montcalm said.

"In that case, let's return to the fort and get started," Passant said.

On the way, he studied Lorena. She saw him looking and smiled.

"What's wrong? Have you never met a vampire before?" she teased.

"I have, in fact. But I have never seen a woman so stunningly beautiful as you, Madame," he replied.

"You have vampires in Canada?" she asked.

"But of course. My cousin, Margaritte, is a vampire. She lives in Montreal. That is where most of them live," Passant replied. "In fact, they have a club called Bloody Mary's on Rue Notre Dam."

"I think I'll pay it a visit," Lorena said.

Hunter smiled.

"Feeling hungry?" he asked.

"A little bit. I can control it a while longer," she said.

"Margaritte told me they serve special cocktails at the club. But when the hunger gets too strong, they find willing donors at the college. I am not so sure what she meant by that," Passant said. "Sometimes, they act as a sort of police auxiliary and hunt down dangerous criminals. I suppose that is what you do, also, in New Orleans."

"It is," she said. "And they never run out of vicious criminals down there."

"Nor up here, Madame. Montreal is quite peaceful as is Quebec," Passant said. "But Msr. Gaude, the Mounted Police chief, could fill you in much better than I can on such matters."

Hunter turned to Montcalm.

"Why didn't you mention there was a vampire community here?" he asked.

"You never asked. Besides, I would hardly call it a community. I think there are less than two dozen vampires in all of Quebec. Since they don't cause us any trouble, we tend to let them be. I imagine there are many more where you're from," Montcalm said.

"Too many to count," Hunter said. "Let's head back to Montreal and plan our strategy. We can eat while we talk."

"I think I'll visit that vampire club," Lorena said. "I'll be back in time to leave with you."

St. Augustine

They reached St. Augustine two hours later. Potter ordered his men to spread out and patrol the streets while he, Rick, Mel and Harper walked back to the Government House. Along the way, they passed the Cathedral and saw Padre Pino waving at them from the steps.

They walked over.

"You should have seen it!," he said. "There were hundreds of balls of bright lights. They streaked through the city streets at great speed. Each light entered a separate house, too. Then all became very quiet. I have never seen anything like it in my entire life!"

"Was anyone hurt?" Potter asked.

"I checked a few of the nearby homes and everyone seemed just fine. Most of the women said they felt very satisfied for some reason. They were all smiling, too," Pino said.

"Those balls of light—orbs—were the spirits of the French soldiers," Rick said.

"I know," Pino nodded.

"But why would they enter peoples' houses?" Potter asked.

"Perhaps what is now written on the east wall of the Government House will give you an answer," Pino said as they walked over to the building.

There, in large letters, were the words:

Nous Renassons.

"It says 'We are reborn'," Mel translated. "I'm not real sure what it means, but I think your nightmare is over. Ribault got what he came here for. Too bad Antonio had to die for something his ancestor did though. The supernatural is never fair. Most of the time, the innocents get the worst of it."

Rick laughed.

"What's so funny?" asked Potter.

"I think I've just figured out what the message means. Think about the other message then tie the two together," Rick said.

Mel stared.

"You don't mean?" he began.

"I could be wrong. We'll know for certain if St. Augustine has a sudden jump in the birth rate in about nine months," Rick said.

One of Potter's men came running up to them. Potter asked what was wrong.

"We went down to the beach to bring our dead back for burial but they're all gone," the man said. "There's not a trace of them anywhere."

Potter nodded.

"They're in the sea," Harper said.

CHAPTER TEN:
Something Else that Goes Bump in the Night

St. Francois

Pike and Dr. Norris went into the village to see Mayor Lamour.

"Is it true? Did you actually kill one of the creatures?" Pike queried.

"I sure did, Captain. It came through that wall over there and I shot it. It died quickly, too. I don't think those things are very strong," she replied.

"Where is the body now?" asked Norris.

"I guess it's still in the cooler at the city morgue. Why?" Lamour asked.

"I would like to see it," Norris said.

"So would I. I want to know what we're up against," Pike added.

"Alright. The morgue is just two streets over. Let's go and have a look," Lamour agreed as she threw on her coat.

There was still several inches of snow on the ground but the sidewalks had been cleared. They reached the morgue and knocked on the beveled glass door. A few seconds later. A bent, white-haired man opened it and nodded.

"Bon jour," he greeted as they entered.

"Bon jour, Barnaby," Lamour said. "We came to look at the creature I shot."

"Ah, yes. A most unusual specimen, if I may say so," Barnaby said as he led them down a long hall to a metal door.

He opened it and they were met by a blast of chilled air. Lamour shivered and pulled her coat around herself a little tighter as they followed him past several storage vaults to the last row. He stopped, opened the door and slid the body out. It was draped with a white sheet which Norris pulled back.

He winced.

"What in the name of God is that?" he asked as they studied the twisted figure.

"It appears to be humanoid," Pike said. "But I've never seen that color before nor eyes so large."

"If these creatures dwell in the dark places beneath the earth, they would need such large eyes in order to see. The skin is the color of flesh after it has been dead for several days," Norris said as he examined it.

"If there is one such creature, there must be more of them," Lamour said. "They can walk right through solid walls and doors as easily as we walk through air. That makes them very dangerous as we have no way to defends ourselves against them."

Pike nodded.

"We sure as Hell can't hide behind locked doors," he said. "But thanks to you, we know they are easily killed. That's something."

They thanked Barnaby and left the morgue.

"What are they, Dr. Norris?" Lamour asked as they walked back to her office.

"All I can say for sure is they dwell underground and eat corpses," he replied. "Anything more and I'd be guessing."

"Have they been seen in other places?" she asked.

"I don't know. The blizzards have cut us off from everyone else. If these things are plaguing other places, I haven't heard about it yet," Pike said.

"Has anyone else come down with this strange ailment since you last reported it to me?" Norris asked.

"Dr. Deaver is the best one to ask about that," Lamour said. "And he hasn't mentioned anything to me lately."

"No news is good news, eh?" Pike smiled.

"Let's hope so, Captain," Lamour said.

New Orleans

The night was dark and moonless and a steady rain pelted the narrow streets of the French Quarter. Alejandro, dressed in his usual flamboyant garb, stepped out of the small bar. Just as he crossed the street, an obviously terrified woman ran past him. He stepped into the shadows of a door way as she sped down Dumaine and waited to see what she was fleeing from.

He didn't have to wait very long.

A long, lean and very muscular humanoid creature with sharp, dog-like facial features and hideous-looking tusks turned the corner and raced after the woman. The creature's gait seemed almost perverse as it rushed past Alejandro.

"It's time," he said as he removed his hat, mask and other clothing and morphed into his rougarou persona. As soon as his transformation was complete, he sped after the creature, which was now two blocks in front of him and quickly closing in on his intended prey. Alejandro watched almost in awe as the creature leaped high into the air and came down directly in front of the woman. She screamed and cringed as it closed in for the kill.

Alejandro ran as fast as he could. The creature was too intent on his prey to hear him. That gave Alejandro a decided edge. He would be able to take the creature completely by surprise.

Or so he thought.

Alejandro pounced.

The creature turned quickly and seized him by the throat. Then he whirled around and threw him. Alejandro soared high into the air and came down in the middle of a pile of restaurant garbage more than a block away. By the time he extricated himself from the rancid rice, fish bones, oyster shells and crawfish remains and other waste, the creature and the woman were gone.

He slowly reverted to human form and looked around. After a few seconds, he scratched his head and wondered what on Earth he had just encountered. He knocked the rice from his hair and retrieved his clothes from the doorway.

"I need another drink," he decided as he dressed and walked down Bourbon Street to the Dragon.

Madison was tending bar when he walked in and sat down in one of the stools.

"I'll have a triple Absinthe and Turbo Dog chaser," he said.

She poured him the drinks and watched as he gulped both down and ordered another round. She refilled his glasses and set them in front of him. He sipped the Absinthe slowly this time. As he drank, he told her what happened.

"You are the only one who has ever bested me in a fight," he said. "But that thing was faster and stronger than anything I have ever met. I have never seen his like before, but now I am determined to find him."

"What happened to the woman?" Madison asked.

"She also vanished into the night. I don't know if she escaped or that thing got her. Neither left a scent I could follow," Alejandro said. "If the woman left a scent, it was a very common one that blends easily into everyone else's."

"What do you plan to do?" Madison asked.

"All I can do now is watch and wait to see if that creature returns," he said as he finished his beer.

"Want me to help?" Madison asked as she refreshed his drinks.

"I would appreciate any assistance you care to provide. Four eyes are better than two. Six are even better," he replied.

"I was thinking the same thing," she agreed. 'Let's drop in and visit Hannah after I get off work."

Three hours later, they stopped by the Emporium. Hannah had just returned from her nightly patrol and invited them inside. Alejandro told her of his encounter.

"What does it look like?" Hannah asked.

"That is most difficult to say," Alejandro replied. "It looks like a large, muscular rougarou with bright green eyes and tusks like a boar."

Hannah tried to envision the creature in her mind. The more she tried, the more dangerous a form it took on.

"What do you suppose it is?" she asked.

"I'll be damned if I know," Alejandro said. "But if it is stalking the streets of New Orleans, we must find it and kill it before it wreaks all sorts of havoc."

Montreal

Marcel Guivre was the owner of the Bloody Mary Night Club. He was broad shouldered, tall and shaved his head. He sported a goatee which was bright red and had thin scar that ran diagonally from just above his left eyebrow to the right hand corner of his upper lip.

Guivre knew every vampire in Montreal as they all frequented the club. When Lorena walked in, she immediately caught his undivided attention. She walked up to the bar and sat down on the stool right in front of him.

"Bon soir, Madame. How may I serve you?" he asked.

"What is your strongest cocktail?" she asked.

"We have a triple Bloody Mary that is quite rich," Guivre said. "It is 25% vodka and 75% blood."

"I will have that, Monsieur," Lorena said with a smile.

"You look a little pallid," he said as he mixed the drink.

"It has been a long time," she said.

"I see. You are new here. Have you recently arrived in Montreal?" Guivre asked.

"Oui. My husband and I are visiting from New Orleans," she replied as he placed the drink before her.

"New Orleans? Oh, you are Madame Hunter. I have heard all about you. You both are well known, even way up here in Canada. Tales of your deeds travel quickly through vampire communities," Guivre said. "May I say that you are even more beautiful than we have heard."

Lorena smiled and handed him her empty glass. He took it and mixed her another cocktail. She noticed the scar on his face.

"That is from a saber," she said. "But we vampires don't scar."

"Ah, but you are very observant, Madame," Guivre said as he handed her the drink. "I acquired this during the battle against the British in 1759. I barely survived the wound, which never healed properly. So I was left with this rather, er, elegant scar."

She laughed.

"So, you weren't a vampire then?" she asked.

"No. I was turned by a remarkably lovely young woman several years later while I was visiting a cousin in New Orleans. He himself, is a vampire. He had been turned by the same exact woman a few years before. Since he enjoyed being a vampire, and he told me of the many advantages he benefited from, I asked him to arrange to have me turned. Perhaps you know my cousin? He owns several clubs in New Orleans," Guivre explained.

"Tony LeFleur is your cousin?" she asked as she handed the empty glass to him.

"Oui. It was he who wrote to tell me about you and Hunter. He claims that you are very close friends," Guivre said with a grin as he handed the refill.

"Oui. We are very good friends. Tony has helped us on several occasions, too," Lorena said. "He never mentioned he had a relative in Canada."

"I am his only living blood relative. We LeFleurs are a vanishing clan. Tony wrote that you and Hunter and your friend DuCassal are considered heroes by the vampires in Louisiana. Isn't that sort of ironic?" Guivre said.

"Very, but understandable given the circumstances," Lorena said. "But my husband and I thought that the statues they erected of us in the City Park were a bit too much and embarrassing. We Slayers like to stay out of public view as much as possible. It took us a while to grow accustomed to our new-found celebrity."

Guivre laughed.

"I can imagine. Does that interfere with your work?" he asked.

"Not really—but we've also become popular with tourists lately. They stop us on the streets to chat, have photos taken with us and autograph their guide books. Our friend, Jean-Paul says we have become almost like rock stars," Lorena said.

"Fame does have its price," Guivre said.

"I have to go now. How much do I owe you?" Lorena asked after she'd had three more.

"Since you are a friend of Tony's, you owe me nothing. The drinks are on the house," Guivre replied.

"That is very kind of you, Monsieur. Merci," Lorena said. "It was a pleasure meeting you."

"The pleasure is all mine, Madame. Please stop by again before you leave Montreal and bring your friends. I would love to meet them," Guivre said with a big grin.

"I will try. Au revoir!" Lorena said as she got up and left.

Guivre watched her walk out and smiled as he put the used glass in the sink.

That evening, they took the ferry to Ft. Stewart.

"How was the vampire club?" Hunter asked.

Lorena shrugged.

"It wasn't much of anything really," she said. "The Bloody Marys are good and strong, so I drank six of them. That should hold me for a while."

"Are you sure?" Hunter asked.

She nodded unconvincingly.

Hunter knew she hadn't fed for a few weeks. Although the cocktails would dull her appetite, sooner or later, she'd need warm, human blood to survive. Neither Montreal or Quebec had a real violent criminal element. In fact, the crimes committed were too petty and hardly ever prosecuted. They were not worth killing anyone over.

She didn't dare feed on the creatures. She had no idea what the virus in their bodies would do to her. She might not be immune to it and she sure as Hell didn't want to become one of them.

Hunter smiled at her.

She smiled back and nodded.

If worse came to worse, she knew he'd allow her to feed on him. To take just enough blood to keep her strength up. She'd done so before, but it left him weak and tired for days afterward and this was neither the time nor place for a Slayer who was not at the peak of his game.

"I'll be alright, mon cher," she said softly.

When they arrived, Passant had his entire company ready for action. He saluted Montcalm.

"We are ready, mon Colonel," he said. "I have already briefed the men and they know their mission and what to expect."

"Lead us to that entrance, Lieutenant," Montcalm said.

They marched out of the fort and along a gravel road to a place in the hills. The door was made of solid steel and rusted in several places. It looked as if it hadn't been opened for years.

"Shall we?" asked Montcalm.

"Let's," Hunter said.

Hunter gripped the handle and pulled. The rusted gate creaked and groaned like a tired ghost as it opened and a rush of stale air followed.

Montcalm and the others watched as Lorena peered inside. She stood quietly and concentrated for a few moments, then turned to Hunter.

"I can hear heartbeats. They are very faint but there," she said.

"Can you tell how many?" Hunter asked.

"A dozen or so at most. They are far back inside," she replied. "They should be very easy to locate."

Montcalm turned to signal his men. Hunter stopped him.

"Your soldiers would make too much noise. The creatures will hear them and flee deeper into the sewers and make it more difficult for us to kill them," he said.

"Then what will you have us do?" Montcalm asked.

"Station a dozen of your men at each entry and give them orders to shoot anyone who tries to get out," Hunter said.

"Except us, of course," DuCassal added. "I would hate to have my new coat ruined by some trigger happy soldier."

Montcalm laughed.

"Then I suggest that you identify yourself before you emerge," he said. He turned to Passant.

"Take one squad to the next entry," he ordered.

Passant saluted and marched off with half the soldiers. The next entry was a half mile away. It would take at least 15 minutes to get there, even at double-time. The others sat back and waited. When 15 minutes lapsed, Hunter, Lorena and DuCassal walked to the entry.

"I'll go first," Lorena said. "I can see in the dark better than you."

Hunter nodded.

"We'll be a few paces behind you. If you run into any of those things, try not to get bitten—and don't bite any of them. We have no way of knowing if any of their strange bacteria can be transmitted to you and I would hate to have you change on me," he said.

"You be just as careful, mon cher," she said as she kissed him.

She stepped into the opening and quickly vanished into the darkness. Montcalm noticed that she didn't make even the slightest sound when she walked.

"Vampires always walk in complete silence," Hunter explained. "That enables them to sneak up on their prey without being detected."

"Do Slayers also walk in silence?" Montcalm asked.

"We can if we concentrate," Hunter replied as he stepped inside.

DuCassal checked his shotgun to be sure it was loaded and followed him. Montcalm watched as they, too, faded into the shadows.

When Passant and his men reached the other entry, they saw that it was still bricked up. The snow around it was still quite deep and it covered almost the entire entry. It looked as if nothing had disturbed the area for years.

He also knew that looks were deceiving. They had told them that the creatures seemed to be able to move through solid walls without leaving tracks. If true, he and his men would have to be fully vigilant when watching the entry so as not to be caught by surprise if any should emerge.

It was still early in the afternoon.

Hunter said the creatures feared sunlight. Perhaps that would keep them from trying to escape until after the sun went down.

He turned to his men.

"This may prove to be a long watch," he said. "It's still quite cold. Feel free to build a fire if you can find twigs that are dry enough to burn. Stay alert and keep your eyes on that wall and shoot anything that tries to get out."

Two of the men went off in search of usable firewood while the others brushed the snow from rocks and stumps to provide themselves with places to rest.

"Just what are we supposed to be looking for, Capitan?" a corporal asked.

"I am not sure. It will look somewhat like a man but more dead than alive. I was told they are dangerous and quite ugly. Do not allow any of them to get close enough to strike or bite you. That is most important. Msr. Hunter said they carry a deadly virus and anyone who gets wounded by them soon becomes one of them," Passant said.

"And you believe him?" the corporal asked.

"Colonel Montcalm backs up his story. If Montcalm says it is true, then we have no choice but to believe," Passant replied. "They both say these creatures can be killed if they are shot in the head. Tell them men to aim for their faces and to keep firing until they are sure the things are dead."

"Oui, Capitan," the corporal said.

Passant smiled as he walked away. He knew that he had just issued what were perhaps the strangest orders his men ever heard.

They walked into the sewer until they were out of sight of the opening. The place reeked of stale water and other unspeakable things and were strangely quiet.

"Notice something missing?" Hunter asked.

"There are no rats down here," DuCassal said. "The average sewer is usually teeming with rats but I have not seen any since we entered."

"Do those things eat rats?" Montcalm asked.

"We don't know," Hunter replied. "It would make some sense. Rats would be a ready and fresh food supply. But all we really know is that creatures eat corpses and anyone bitten by one becomes one of them."

As they turned a corner, Lorena held up her hand. They stopped. Hunter and DuCassal walked over to her. Lorena nodded at a narrow crack in the sewer wall. Several blocks of masonry had been chiseled free and lay scattered on the floor in front of the opening. The stench coming from the crack was nearly overpowering.

"Do you hear?" she whispered.

"Heartbeats," Hunter said. "Several of them. I also hear shallow breathing."

"This crack goes deep into the hillside. Let's find out how deep," DuCassal said as he pointed his flare gun into the crack and fired.

The missile hissed into the darkness then exploded into a wave of bright, blue light which continued into the crack. Seconds later, painful howls and wails emanated from the darkness as the bright light blinded the creatures hiding within. The waited as they screaming creatures shuffled toward the opening. When the first of them stuck its twisted face out of the crack, Hunter fired his revolver into it at point blank range. The creature's face exploded into bits of blood, bone and flesh and it fell back into the crack. His second shot killed the one immediately behind it. He stepped back as a mob of them rushed the opening and watched as DuCassal blasted one apart with his shot gun. Then he stepped aside and allowed the soldiers to finish off the rest.

As the flare burned away, the noises ceased. They waited but no more of the creatures appeared.

"Shall we go in?" asked Montcalm.

"The flare's gone down. It's pitch black inside," DuCassal said as he reloaded his shotgun.

They heard several shots from the group just ahead of them. Montcalm pointed at the three of his men. They nodded and walked in the direction of the shots to join the fight. DuCassal checked the oil level of his lantern and smiled.

"Follow me," he said as he stepped through the crack.

Lorena and Hunter were right on his heels. Montcalm followed with two of his soldiers while the others watched the tunnels. The lantern cast an eerie glow on the passageway which appeared to have been clawed through the hill. The place reeked of urine, feces and rotting flesh and their boots made crunching sounds as they traveled further in.

DuCassal stopped and shone the lantern on the ground. He winced when he saw the half-gnawed human bones and skulls that were scattered everywhere.

"This is where they dispose of the bones after they've stripped the flesh from them," Lorena said.

"It is also their toilet," Montcalm observed as he held his nose.

After walking about 75 feet, they reached a dead end and turned around to rejoin the rest of the company outside the crack. The soldiers were calmly leaning on their rifles when they emerged.

"The shots have ceased," one of the men said.

"Let's find the others," Hunter said as they headed down the main sewer tunnel.

When they turned a corner, they came upon several dead creatures and pools of blood on the ground. There were spent shells everywhere but no sign of the men. A second later, more shots rang out in quick succession and they sped off to see what was happening. They soon reached a large, open area where the lead platoon was busy putting the finishing touches on several more creatures that were writing on the floor in agony while clawing at their molten eyes. A sergeant walked up to Montcalm and saluted. He returned it.

"Report!" he said.

"We were attacked by two separate groups of those things. The first was quite small. I think they numbered less than a dozen. This one was larger. We killed most of them but a few managed to flee further into the sewer. We suffered no casualties. No one got so much as a scratch," the sergeant said.

"Well done, Sergeant," Montcalm smiled.

Lorena pointed straight ahead.

"I sense many in the distance. They are waiting for us in several places," she said.

"Let us not disappoint them, eh?" Montcalm said. "I want four lanterns in front and two to the rear. Keep your eyes and ears open and whatever happens, do not let those things get close enough to bite or scratch you."

The battle, if one can call it that, quickly turned into a complete farce. The creatures attempted to attack only to be nearly crippled by the gleam from the lanterns. As they covered their burning eyes, they became easy targets for the soldiers, who gunned them down by the scores. The creatures offered almost no resistance. Some attempted to flee only to be run down and killed by Hunter, DuCassal and Lorena.

The slaughter continued until the soldiers found themselves at the metal gates of the opposite end of the sewers after leaving a trail of dead, mangles creatures in their wake.

Hunter turned to Lorena.

"Do you hear anything?" he asked.

"I hear only our own hearts beating now, mon cher," she replied. "The battle is ended."

"I counted over 100 of those things," DuCassal said. "That's more than I expected."

"I did not see where they might have entered the sewers from," Montcalm said.

"Since they can walk through solid walls, they probably entered the same way we did," Hunter said as he knocked on the metal gates to signal the soldiers standing guard on the other side.

A moment later, the heavy, rusted gates creaked open and a gust of clean, fresh air wafted into the sewer.

"Ah, that feels nice!" Montcalm remarked as they walked out into the sunlight.

They shut the gates behind them and went back to the fort to discuss further plans. Valons and Dr. Abraham were also there.

"Now that you've cleared out their nest, should I have my men brick up the entrances to the sewers?" Passant asked.

"I think that would be a waste of time, Lieutenant," Montcalm replied. 'Those things can walk through walls without much effort."

"Lights would keep them away," Hunter said. "Can you get someone to string lights all through the sewers?"

"I will speak with our engineers," Valons said. "I'm sure it can be done."

"In the meantime, I will have my men patrol the sewers on a regular basis," Passant said.

"And tell them to stay alert. I might also suggest that you continue to cremate your dead to keep those things from eating them. Patrol the villages, too. Those things could return at any time," Montcalm said.

St. Augustine

The next morning, Rick and Mel walked over to the Government House to speak with Potter. They found him seated behind Lopez's desk and going through a stack of files. Alicia, Lopez's daughter, was nowhere to be seen.

"I've got those numbers for you. We had eight killed on the beach and five more in the city. The five in the city had been drowned like the others. I'm willing to bet that all of them descendants of the Spanish soldiers that committed the massacre," Potter said.

He sipped his coffee.

"Funny how they didn't kill any women," he said.

"It isn't if you think about the messages Ribault left," Mel said. "They didn't kill any women because they had need of them."

"For what?" Potter asked.

"Incubators," Rick said with a grin. "I'd say that right now, there are 270 very pregnant women here in St. Augustine."

"That's crazy!" Potter said.

"That's the supernatural," Mel said with a smile. "By the way, where's Alicia?"

"She was here a little while ago but had to leave because she felt sick. She said she woke up feeling sick this morning," Potter explained.

He sat back and looked at them. Then all three broke into laughter.

"Well, this could be a blessing in disguise. We can use some new blood in this city. It's been a long time since we had a spike in births here," Potter said.

"Only time will tell," Rick said as they shook hands.

Montreal

They returned to Montreal on the next ferry. Since they had not eaten for most of the day, they headed right for the nearest restaurant

As Hunter and company sat down to eat their lunch, Gaude and Bourgue walked over, pulled up chairs and sat down. The mayor looked tired. Gaude looked puzzled.

"While you were gone, I sent half my men down into the UPN to be sure it was clear and to search for any possible ways into or out of the network that we are not aware of. After twelve hours, they have found nothing," Gaude said.

Hunter sipped his coffee and nodded.

"But there has to be something. Those things did not just materialize down there," Gaude said in frustration.

"Do you think they will return?" the mayor asked.

"Not as long as you keep the lights on and repair the ones that are out. After seeing what light does to them, I can understand why they fear it. I would, too, if it melted my eyeballs," Hunter said.

"Ft. Stewart is also safe for now," DuCassal added. "I don't think Passant believed us until he actually saw those things."

The others laughed.

"The only sure way to keep them from returning is to locate the main lair and exterminate every last one of them," Montcalm said.

"Or find out who or what's really behind this and eliminate that," Hunter said. "Creatures like these don't just show up out of the blue to infest a place. Something or someone brought them here. There's a purpose to this. A very dark, evil purpose."

"Discover the purpose and that might lead us to whoever is behind this," Lorena said.

"That's the only way we can eliminate the problem," Hunter added.

Quebec

LeVant and Marquand were waiting as their boat glided up to the side of the pier. Hunter saw the expressions on their faces.

"What's wrong?" he asked.

"Those things are becoming bolder," Marquand said. "Last night, at least 20 of them attempted to scale the wall near Porte St. Jean. The guards spotted them and sounded the alarm. None of them got inside and no one was hurt in the skirmish."

"The soldiers killed five and wounded several others. But that wasn't the end of it," LeVant said as they walked toward the Batterie Royal.

"An hour before sunrise, another group of those things were sighted here in the Vieux Port. A squad of our men chased them along the waterfront until they vanished at dawn. No one was injured," Marquand said.

"Interesting. It seems like they were probing the defenses for weaknesses," Montcalm said.

"Exactly," Hunter said. "This confirms my suspicions. Someone is guiding those things. Someone highly intelligent. They're preparing for a major attack on the city."

"In effect, we are at war now," Montcalm said.

"You've been at war ever since the first corpse was eaten. You just didn't know it," Hunter said. "I suggest that you double the guard from now on."

"Hell, I'll triple it!" Montcalm assured him.

The night did not pass quietly. The creatures made several attempts to enter city at different places. Each time, they were shot to pieces by Montcalm's soldiers and sent running.

The raids started right after sundown and continued every few minutes until dawn. At one point, a large group of them assailed the small fort at the base of the city wall in Place Royale. A handful even managed to get inside and grapple with the defenders. But when all was said and done, all of the creatures lay dead.

At sunrise, Montcalm held a roll call. Duchesne reported two men missing and two wounded and at least five dozen creatures killed.

Montcalm looked at Hunter who was standing next to him. He'd and his companions had been up all night, fighting side-by-side with his soldiers. Hunter had directed the defense for the most part and his skillful placement of men and quick response times had kept the creatures out of Quebec.

"What should we do with our wounded?" Montcalm asked.

"I suggest you place them into a cell and put a guard on them. The minute they begin changing, shoot them," Hunter said.

"You want me to shoot my own men?" Montcalm asked.

"It's either that or you'll end up killing them later when they come back to kill you," Hunter replied. "If you don't shoot them, I will."

One of the wounded men stepped forward. He drew his pistol and placed it against his temple.

"Au revoir, mes amis!" he said as he pulled the trigger.

They winced as his head erupted and he tumbled to the ground. The second man looked at Hunter. He drew his weapon and handed it to him.

"I would prefer that you shoot me now, Monsieur," he said. "It is the only thing left for me now."

Hunter stepped back. He pointed the pistol at him.

"I wish there was another way," he said as he pulled the trigger.

When the man hit the ground, Hunter made the sign of the cross.

Montcalm turned to Duchesne.

"Have these men cremated and bring their personal effects to my office afterward, Sergeant Major," he ordered.

Duchesne saluted.

CHAPTER ELEVEN: Reinforcements

Noon.

The Star of Canada glided slowly into its berth in the Vieux Port. On deck with the other passengers were two tall young men dressed in the unmistakable black garb of Slayers. When they walked down the gangplank to the pier, Hunter. Lorena, DuCassal and Montcalm greeted them. Hunter made the introductions.

Mel smiled as he shook hands with Lorena.

"So we finally get to meet you," he said. "I must say that you're far more beautiful than I ever imagined. No wonder Hunter lost his heart to you."

Lorena smiled.

"Merci, Carmello," she said.

"Call me Mel. That's what everyone in Savannah calls me and I've gotten used to it," he said.

"And I'm Rick," his brother said.

"Sounds like you've been adopted," DuCassal said.

"You could say that," Mel said. "We've both married local girls. They're sisters. In fact, they're the sheriffs' daughters."

"It wasn't a shotgun wedding, was it?" DuCassal asked as they walked to Montcalm's carriage.

"You know, I'm not exactly sure. Before we knew it, we were married. We even bought houses," Rick said.

"Haunted, of course," Mel added.

"Of course!" Hunter smiled. "How was St. Augustine?"

"Harrowing," Mel replied. "What's been going on up here? Why does the Cardinal feel that all of us need to be here?"

They climbed into the carriage. On the way to the hotel, Hunter explained what was going on. Both listened quietly until he'd finished.

"Werewolves?" Mel asked.

"No. I'm not sure what they are. All I know is that they eat corpses and kidnap the living. I've never encountered anything like them and I've encountered more strange creatures in my lifetime than I can even count," Hunter said.

"Another thing: anyone who gets bitten or scratched by these things turns into one of them. And they are becoming very bold and aggressive. They have even managed to wipe almost an entire company of my soldiers," Montcalm said. "Whatever they are, they are ravaging Quebec."

"Then there's the strange illness that's going around. Whoever gets it, dies in a few days," Hunter said.

"The plague?" Rick asked.

"Oui. It began back in late September. As the weather grew colder, it spread more quickly. None of our doctors has been able to identify or treat it. And it is always fatal," Montcalm said.

The brothers looked at each other.

"That explains why the Cardinal sent us all up here," Mel said. "This is quite an unusual case."

"It's completely different than anything else I've ever experienced," Hunter said.

"It almost sounds like someone really has it in for the people of Quebec," Rick said.

"You mean like a curse of some sort?" Lorena asked.

Rick nodded.

"Why not? In our business, we can't rule anything out," he said.

"I've thought of that, Rick. But we can't come up with a logical reason for it," Hunter said. "Nor can anyone else."

"You've arrived at the right time," Montcalm said. "The ice is almost gone from the river and the roads are becoming more passable. Travel will be easier for us from now on."

"And for those things as well," Hunter added.

Although the night was filled with those eerie howls, there were no incidents reported. Hunter and DuCassal watched as the guard changed shifts, then headed back to the hotel. They cleaned up and headed downstairs for breakfast. Lorena was already seated and waiting. They walked over and sat down.

"I patrolled Place Royale all night. It was very quiet. I think it's because the area was well-lit with street lamps. Those things are very fearful of the light," she explained. "When the sun came up, I returned to the hotel and took a long, hot shower before coming down here. How was your night?"

"Pretty much the same," Hunter said.

"Those things were out there but they made no attempt to enter the city," DuCassal added. "I thought that was very strange."

"It's almost like they're waiting for something," Hunter said.

"Or some*one*," DuCassal said as he poured himself a cup of hot coffee.

While they ate, two young Native Americans entered the restaurant and looked around. They spotted Hunter and walked over to the table.

"Are you the one called Hunter?" the taller boy asked.

"Yes," Hunter said as he put down his fork.

"My name is Johnny Bright Moon. This is my brother, Sam," the boy said. "We've come from Wendake to see you."

"Why?" Hunter asked.

"Our uncle, Two Feathers, sent us to find you. He said to tell you that if you want to know who is behind the troubles, you should come to Wendake and speak with him," Bright Moon said.

"Our uncle is the tribal shaman. He knows *everything*," Sam boasted.

"How do we get there?" Hunter asked.

The taller boy reached into his jacket pocket and took out a folded paper. He handed it to Hunter. It was a hand drawn map. He nodded.

"Tell your uncle we'll be there tomorrow night," he said.

The boys nodded and hurried from the restaurant without saying another word. Hunter smiled.

"Wendake is about 15 miles to the north and west of Quebec," he explained.

"Charles and I have been there many times before. Mostly before the British took over," DuCassal added. "It's good to know that the Huron still retain their ancestral homelands."

Hunter nodded.

"Not many Nations were able to do that. The Huron are one of the exceptions, mostly because they became valuable trading partners to both the French and English. They've always been good business people," he said.

"Sounds like an interesting trip. When do we leave?" Rick asked.

"Right after breakfast. It should take us about ten hours to reach the First Nations area," Hunter said.

It took them the better part of the day to reach Wendake, the ancient home of the people the Quebecois called the Hurons. They called themselves Wendat but they didn't mind the Huron tag. After all, the Whites had been calling them by that name for centuries.

Wendake was a land of deep forests, ice-capped peaks, pristine rivers and crystal clear lakes about 20 miles to the north and east of Quebec. The Great Disaster passed unnoticed by the Wendat. The fall of the White Man's civilization was of little concern to the First People. They had been there long before the first European set boots on their soil. They would still be there long after the last White Man left.

The Wendat had retained their traditions and culture. They lived by farming, hunting, fishing and selling meats and other goods to the Quebecois—just as they had since the 1600s of the First Age. They never took from the land more than they needs and they always thanked the spirits of the animals they killed for food.

Had it not been for the Wendat, the Quebecois might not have survived the Dark Years after the Great Disaster. Their warriors helped protect the northern frontiers from would-be invaders and they provided most of the fresh meat and some crops that were vital to the Quebecois' survival.

George Two Feathers Benoit, was the most powerful shaman of the Wendat Nation. He was well-learned in the ancient traditions and lore and well-respected as a healer and seer. Two Feathers stood over six feet tall and wore his gray streaked hair in the traditional braids. He always dressed in buckskins and tall moose hide boots. And he wore a protective amulet around his neck.

Two Feathers knew all there was to know about herbs, smoke and mushrooms. It was said that he knew or remembered things that other shaman had long forgotten.

He was seated in a high backed chair in front of the fireplace, watching the flames crackle and dance amid the logs as he smoked his pipe when he heard horses stop just outside his small house. He watched as Hunter eased the door open and peeked inside, then nodded and motioned for them to enter.

"Come in and make yourselves comfortable," he greeted. "I've been expecting you.

He smiled at Hunter as he sat down across from him.

"I'm glad my nephews found you," he said. "The older wishes to follow in my footsteps but I'm not sure he is cut out for the job. The younger desires to become a great hunter. He will probably reach his goals."

He paused, puffed his pipe and blew a cloud of smoke into the air. He smiled at Lorena.

"You're a vampire," he said. "I sense that you have not fed in a long while."

Lorena nodded.

Two Feathers smiled.

"I think you will be able to satisfy your hunger before this night is ended," he said. "Of course, that's just a hunch on my part."

He laughed at their expressions.

"Tell me about the troubles in Quebec," he said.

Hunter went into great detail about all that had happened in the various places they'd visited. He also described the strange, corpse-eating creatures in detail. The entire time, Two Feathers sat quietly and listened as he puffed his pipe.

"I hope you can tell us what we're up against," Hunter said. "The problem seems to be spreading to the entire province."

Two Feathers puffed on his pipe as he gazed into the flames. After giving the matter some careful thought, he nodded.

"I am a very old man. The Raven already perches outside my door, waiting to take my soul to the Great Spirit. So in this, the winter of my long life, it matters little to me when my time on this Earth comes to an end," he said.

He took another puff and blew a smoke ring above their heads. The ring swirled around until it formed the outline of a large eagle then slowly dispersed. Two Feathers smiled at their reaction.

"The legends of our people tell of a being. They say to speak her name brings death. I say it is time to learn if those legends hold any truth," he said.

"Those creatures you speak of are called the Apotamkin. The stories about them have been passed down among my people since the beginning of time.

It is said they live deep beneath the earth in dimly lit caverns and tunnels. The Apotamkin are a form of earth demon who feed upon the recently buried or take blood from the living much like vampires. They hate and fear light of any kind and sunlight weakens them and makes them easier to kill. It is said they travel at night in packs and anyone bitten by them becomes an Apotamkin in a few days. They also kidnap the living, both to take blood from them and to add to their numbers," he concluded.

"That fits those things perfectly," Hunter said.

Two Feathers puffed on his pipe again. As he exhaled, the image of a grayish humanoid being with extended gnarled fingers and nails appeared.

"Is this what you saw?" he asked.

"Yes. That's it exactly," Hunter said.

"The Apotamkin are intelligent and very vicious by nature. They despise humans and consider us only as a source of food," Two Feathers explained.

"How do we deal with them?" asked DuCassal.

"Light immobilizes them. A bullet to the skull will kill them, as will a strike from a silver weapon. Prolonged exposure to strong sunlight will turn them into dust," Two Feathers said. "But even though the Apotamkin are many and their numbers continue to grow, they are not what you should fear most."

Hunter looked at him.

"There's someone controlling them, isn't there?" he asked. "Is it the one whose name brings death to whomever speaks it?"

Two Feathers nodded.

"Who is she?" asked Lorena.

Two Feathers took a long puff and slowly exhaled the smoke.

"She goes by many names," he said. ":My people call her the Cold Lady."

"Is she also a demon?" Mel asked.

"No. She is far worse than any demon you can ever imagine. She is tall, sexy. Beautiful enough to steal your breath away. Her hair is very long and snow white. Her skin is pale and nearly colorless. Sometimes it looks pale blue. Her eyes are a paler blue.

She comes from a frozen land that is part of the Earth but not on it. She is dead yet alive. She dwells between darkness and light and can change her shape and appearance at will. She is also cold hearted, ruthless and more evil than any creature that walks. She hates all warm, living things because she is condemned to live apart from them until the end of time.

It is she who controls the Apotamkin.

It is she who sends them to plague the people of this country, although I do not her reason. Destroy the Cold Lady and the Apotamkin will die with her," Two Feathers said.

"How?" Hunter asked.

Two feathers smiled.

"You know we Natives never say that," he joked.

The others chuckled.

"To slay the Cold Lady, you must shoot her in the heart with an arrow made from the branches of the sacred willow," Two Feathers said.

"Where does this willow grow?" asked Hunter.

"Far to the north and east, in the deepest part of the forest of the First Nations," Two Feathers said.

"How will we know if we've found the right tree?" asked Rick.

"That's easy. It will be bleeding," Two Feathers said.

Just then, a sudden wind blew the door wide open and filled the room with a powerful, almost numbing chill. Two Feathers gripped his chest, smiled at Hunter and slumped back in his chair. Hunter checked his pulse as the chill quickly diminished.

"He's dead," Hunter said. "He died right after he spoke her name. Just like the legends said."

"But you also spoke her name, mon cher. Yet you still live," Lorena said.

"A curse only works if you truly believe in it," Hunter said. "And Two feathers believed. Let's tell the others so they can give him a proper funeral."

He saw that familiar look in her eyes and nodded.

"Go ahead. He doesn't need it anymore and I'm sure he won't mind," he said.

She waited until he led the others out of the house and shut the door behind him. She looked at the still warm body of Two Feathers and rolled back her hood.

A few minutes later, she exited the house feeling energized. She wiped the traces of blood from her lips with a handkerchief and smiled at Hunter. He smiled back as they mounted their horses and rode away from the house.

Mel looked at Lorena.

"What's wrong?" she asked.

"I thought that vampires only fed on living things," he said.

"Under normal circumstances, we do. But in places where victims aren't readily available, like here, we must resort to alternative sources of nourishment. We can feed on the dead as long as the body is still fresh and warm and it hasn't begun to decompose. Since Two Feathers had been dead only a few seconds, he was perfect," she explained. "I tried the cocktail at the vampire club and they did help a little. But in the end, a girl's got to feed."

"How long can you go without feeding?" Rick asked.

"Two or three weeks if I force myself," Lorena said. "This is the first time I've ever fed on a corpse. I hope I don't have to do it again."

"Oh? Why is that?" asked DuCassal.

"Even though the body was still fresh, his blood had a slightly bitter taste to it," she replied. "I prefer blood that's fresh and sweet."

Hunter and DuCassal laughed.

Mel and Rick glanced at each other and shrugged.

"Do you have any sisters?" Rick joked.

"Not that I know of," Lorena said.

"Too bad," he said.

"I thought you said that you were married," Lorena teased.

"I am. But I man can dream, can't he?" Rick responded.

Lorena laughed. So did Hunter and DuCassal.

"You know, his description of the Cold Lady reminds me of a woman you and I knew a long time ago," DuCassal said as they left the house.

"The White Witch of Rose Hall?" Hunter asked.

DuCassal smiled and nodded.

"Now she was a real piece of work, eh, Charles?" he said as they mounted their horses.

"Whatever became of Annie?" Hunter asked.

"Her slaves killed her while she slept. As the years passed, everyone involved in her murder came to most horrible ends. The members of succeeding generations supposedly suffered similar fates. It is said that she put a curse on them that is still working to this very day," DuCassal said.

'And Rose Hall?" Hunter asked.

"During the First Age, it was famous as a very haunted luxury hotel. I do not know what became of it later," DuCassal said. "Jamaica is a place I have not thought to visit for a very long time."

"Jamaica?" Lorena asked.

"No—but I tried many times," DuCassal joked.

Hunter laughed.

"It's one of the largest islands in the Caribbean. Jean-Paul and I frequented the city of Port Royal during our buccaneering days," Hunter said.

"You were a pirate?" Lorena asked.

"I prefer privateer," Hunter said.

"We sailed under many different flags, Lorena," DuCassal said. "The countries we worked for called us privateers. The ones we preyed upon called us pirates. It is a matter of perspective—and profits."

"The more I learn about you, the more I am surprised," Lorena smiled.

"Sometimes it surprises me, too," Hunter said.

"Two Feathers failed to answer the most important question about the Cold Lady," Mel said.

Hunter nodded.

"If she's a demon, then someone had to have summoned her to our world," he said.

"Exactly!" Mel nodded.

"And whoever did it really has it in for the Quebecois," Rick added.

"Two Feathers also said that she wasn't like any demon we've ever known. If that's the case, perhaps no one summoned her. Perhaps she came here of her own volition to exact some sort of revenge," Hunter pointed out.

"Now what, mes amis?" asked DuCassal.

"We head north and find that tree," Hunter said.

"How do we find a single tree in such a vast forest?" Rick asked as they looked up at the mountains.

"If you were a vampire it would be easy," Lorena said. "You'd just follow your nose. We can smell blood within a square mile. If that tree does actually bleed, I'll find it."

They followed a twisting path through the forest. It took them northward in a meandering way. They rode past beautiful snow covered mountains and across crystal clear streams. The entire region was still blanked by several inches of snow and this made travel slow and difficult. As they crossed another stream and entered a wide glen, they stopped.

"What's wrong?" Hunter asked as Lorena looked around.

"That tree is nearby," Lorena said. "I can smell fresh blood."

"How close?" asked Hunter.

"Less than a mile. But with this wind, I can't tell what direction," Lorena said.

"There are two paths up ahead," DuCassal said.

"Let's split up. We can cover more ground that way. You and Rick travel the left fork. We'll take the right. Keep alert. If that tree is as sacred as Two Feathers said, it's bound to be well-guarded by something," Hunter said.

Mel nodded.

"We'll send up a flare if we run into anything. You do the same. Good luck," he said as he and Rick rode off.

Quebec.

Montcalm was talking with Marquand in the Governor-General's office when Duchesne rushed in to inform them that at least 20 fishing boats and one ferry loaded with people, had arrive at the Vieux Port.

"Where are they from?" Marquand asked.

"Ste. Petronille," Duchesne said.

They hurried down to the docks and watched as hundreds of people disembarked. There were five haggard-looking soldiers with them. Sgt. Zender spotted Montcalm and walked up. He saluted. Montcalm returned it.

"Report, sergeant," he said.

"These are the people of Ste. Petronille, Sir. We were forced to abandon the village when we were attacked during the night by the strangest creatures I have ever seen," Zender said.

"Attacked?" Montcalm asked.

"Oui, mon colonel. There were at least a hundred of them. They appeared in the middle of the night and attacked anyone they saw. We fought until we were completely out of ammunition. We were about to lose the battle, but the sun came up and those things vanished," Zender replied.

A tall, bald-headed man walked up and introduced himself as Frank Brooks, the mayor of Ste. Petronille. He gave a similar account of the attack.

"We decided to abandon the village in case those things decided to return. Most of my people have family in Quebec they can stay with until the village is made safe. It seemed like the wisest thing to do," Brooks said.

"I lost one man to those things, Sir. Corporal DeMenil," Zender said.

"Have any of your people been injured by those things?" Marquand asked.

"There are at least a dozen," Brooks reported.

"They will have to be quarantined. I will explain later," Marquand replied.

Montcalm scowled.

"That's the second place we have lost to those monsters," he said bitterly. "They are becoming bolder by the day."

"Or more desperate," Marquand said. "Have you heard from St. Francois?"

"Not a word," Montcalm said.

"We must not allow another village to fall to those things. Prepare a company for travel. You leave for St. Francois at sunrise," Marquand instructed.

Lorena rode a head of the others. She followed a narrow path deeper and deeper into the woods. As she rode, the scent grew stronger and stronger. Her nose led her into a cluster of ancient pines situated between two low hills. In the midst of the pines, she saw a most unusual type of tree.

It appeared to be a cross between a weeping willow and a pine. Its trunk was straight and smooth but its branches drooped like a willow. Each branch had several long, slender offshoots that nearly touched the ground but all were covered in dark green pine needles.

To Lorena, it looked like a very depressed Christmas tree.

She dismounted and walked over to it. The scent of blood was powerful now. She looked at the trunk and saw a dark, red sap oozing from it. She ran her fingers through the liquid then tasted it.

"Human blood!" she said. "But how?"

She watched as Hunter and DuCassal caught up to her.

"This is it!" she said as she held up her fingers to show them the blood.

Hunter took out his flare gun and fired it. The O'Sheas saw the sparkling light and rushed toward it. They arrived five minutes later.

"What kind of tree is *that*?" asked Mel as he rode closer.

"It doesn't matter. This is the one we want," Hunter said as he dismounted.

He selected a fairly straight, strong branch and lopped it off with his Bowie knife. To everyone's shock, the tree emitted a long, high-pitched scream that caused them to cover their ears.

"Look!" Mel said as he pointed to the spot where the branch had been cut.

They stared in wonder when the saw that the tree was now bleeding profusely. And it was trembling as if it were in pain.

Without warning, it suddenly lashed out at Rick and knocked him from his saddle. Instinctively, DuCassal fired both barrels into the trunk. The wood splintered and flew in all directions as the tree screamed in agony and shook violently. Then it emitted a deep, mournful groan.

They gaped in disbelief as the tree vanished, leaving a naked young Indian maiden in its place. Hunter hurried to her side and turned her over. She looked up at him and smiled. Then the light left her eyes. He laid her back down and made the sign of the cross. They watched as she slowly vanished into thin air.

"Who do you think she was?" asked Rick.

"She was probably some poor woman who crossed a powerful witch and got turned into a tree so she could suffer forever," Hunter said. "When we killed the tree, he soul was freed."

"Do you suppose the Cold Woman did that to her?" DuCassal asked.

"Your guess is as good as anyone's, Jean-Paul," Hunter said as he mounted his horse. "Let's get back to Quebec. I have an arrow to make."

It was early morning when they reached Quebec. The sun was just climbing above the wooded mountains to the east and the entire region was cast in a deceptive orange glow. They took the road up to the Porte Palais. The two soldiers on the wall saw them ride up and shouted to the men below to open the gate. They waited as the heavy wooden doors creaked open and entered the city.

As they dismounted, half-dozen Guards ran up to them.

"Why was the gate closed?" Hunter asked.

"We were attacked, Monsieur," one Guard replied.

"Attacked?" Hunter asked.

"Oui. Those things got inside the city last night. Colonel Montcalm called out the entire regiment to repel them. We just finished off the last of them an hour ago," the soldier said.

"Where's Montcalm?" asked Hunter.

"I last saw him at Place D'Arms," the soldier said.

As they hurried over to the square, they passed several bodies lying in the streets. Most of them were dead creatures. Some were soldiers. Most had suffered horrifying deaths.

They found Montcalm seated on a bench at the edge of the plaza. He smiled as they approached.

"It was a Hell of a fight. Too bad you missed it," he said.

"How'd they get in?" asked Hunter as they sat down next to him.

"Through one of the side doors of Porte St. Louis," Montcalm replied.

"You mean they broke in?" DuCassal asked.

Montcalm shrugged.

"I have not had the chance to investigate," he said. "If they did break in, one of the four men in the tower would most certainly have heard them. Yet no one knew they were inside the city until one of my patrols spotted them on St. Louis. And sounded the alarm. I ordered every man in the regiment to repel them. There were dozens of those things. They seemed to be everywhere, too."

"Let's have a look at that gate," Hunter said.

They got up and walked to the gate.

"What about casualties?" Hunter asked.

"I won't know until later this afternoon when I receive the reports. I can tell you that it was bad. Really bad," Montcalm replied.

When they reached the gate, they saw it was still closed. Several tired-looking soldiers stood guard around it. Some saluted Montcalm when they approached.

"I believe they entered through the smaller door on the left," Montcalm said as he pointed.

They saw that the door was wide open. Hunter and DuCassal examined it while the O'Sheas looked around on the outside.

"There are no prints," Rick said.

"Those things never leave prints," Lorena reminded him. "Not even in snow."

"That's impossible. If they have any physical substance to them at all, they have to leave prints," Mel said. "Every living creature on Earth leaves prints."

"Not those things," Lorena said.

"There's no signs of forced entry. No splintered wood or chipped stone. Nothing at all," Rick said as he examined the outer door.

They walked back through and watched as Hunter finished his examination. He shook his head.

"This gate was not forced open," he said.

"Then how did they get inside?" Montcalm asked.

Hunter looked at him.

"Two ways. We know those things can walk through solid objects, but I'm not sure they would try such a thing en masse. That would be doing it the hard way and it would take too long," he said.

"I agree. What is the second way?" Montcalm asked.

"The one you're not going to like," Hunter said. "This gate was left open on purpose. Someone inside Quebec unlocked it to enable those things to enter."

Montcalm blanched at the implications.

"Who in their right mind would even dream of such a thing?" he asked.

"Someone who is in contact with those things. Perhaps, the very person who is controlling them," Hunter replied.

He looked at the others.

"This attack was pre-planned. Those things knew which gate would be left open and at what time. That means there's someone inside Quebec who coordinated it," he said.

"Any idea who that could be?" Montcalm asked.

"I have one suspect in mind," Hunter replied as they walked back toward Auberge du Tresor. "I'll tell you all about over dinner tonight."

"Why wait?" asked Montcalm.

"For one, we've had a long, difficult journey back to Quebec. We need to clean up and get some rest. For another, I have to make something," Hunter answered.

"What?" asked Montcalm.

"An arrow," Hunter replied.

As Hunter was about to quit his evening patrol, he spotted a caped figure making its way through the narrow streets. As he watched, he saw it was the same woman who had claimed the body of her husband.

He decided to follow her.

Just as he expected, she led him to the cemetery outside the city walls. She stopped and looked around as if to make certain no one could see her, then opened the gate and went inside. He waited a few seconds then followed.

Hunter followed her deep inside the cemetery. She walked along a winding path that took her past rows of ornate tombs, ancient, moss-stained headstones and leaning monuments. The path took her to furthest corner of the cemetery where she stopped at the base of a small rise. Nestled between the leafless was a solitary headstone. A simple, granite marker.

He watched as she walked up to the grave, stared at it for a few seconds, then knelt down next to it with her head down.

He readied his bow and knocked the arrow to it. He raised it and drew back on the string. He was about to let loose when he realized Rowen was sobbing. Curious, he lowered the bow and walked over to her. She didn't bother to look up. She just continued to weep.

Hunter knelt beside her.

"He was the only one I ever truly loved," she said in a voice that was barely audible and filled with despair. "This is all her doing."

"The Cold Woman?" he asked.

She nodded.

"She is my mother and she is every bit the monster the Wendat say she is. She is a cruel, heartless monster," she said.

"Did she open the gate?" Hunter asked.

"No. I did that. I had no choice. She still has some measure of control over me at times. Most of the time, I can block her. But I have not been able to break free from her altogether. Not yet," Rowen replied sadly.

She looked at the arrow.

"You can kill me if you wish. My life is nothing but ashes now. My joy, my love, has been stolen from me. I don't want to live anymore. I don't want to live without my Andre," she said.

"Your mother is on this rampage because she objected to your marriage?" Hunter asked.

"Oui. I did not think she would take her anger out on everyone in Quebec because of that. I thought she would be happy because I was happy. I was wrong. So terribly wrong. I am truly sorry for what I have caused," she said sobbing.

Hunter put his arm around her.

"I'm not going to harm you, Rowen. You've been hurt enough. Maybe too much," he said. "Killing you won't put an end to this madness anyway."

"I fear that you are right, Msr. Hunter. My mother will not rest until everyone in Quebec has been killed or turned into one of her horrid servants. To end this, you must kill her," Rowen said. "It is the only way."

She broke down and sobbed uncontrollably. He held her closer to comfort her.

"What a terrible price everyone paid because I fell in love!" she lamented.

They knelt there for several minutes. When Rowen composed herself, she wiped her eyes with a handkerchief and looked up at him.

Her eyes now burned with hatred.

"My mother must be killed. This must end. I will help you find her. I want her to pay for what she has done," she said.

Hunter helped her stand and led her away from the grave. He knew she was telling the truth.

"Do you have a father?" he asked.

"No. I was not conceived like a human is conceived. I was created from the boughs of the same tree as you made your arrow from. I think she created me because she was lonely. Or perhaps she just wanted to have someone she cold torment whenever the mood struck her," Rowen said. "Does that matter?"

"Not at all," Hunter assured her. "Did Andre know?"

"I told him the moment we met. He said it did not matter. He didn't care who or what I was as long as we loved each other. He proposed to me on our second date. Of course, I accepted. He was handsome, and brave and gallant and filled with passion. He was everything I ever wanted. Now he's gone and I want the one who took him from me dead," Rowen said bitterly.

When they entered the 1640, DuCassal, Lorena and the O'Sheas were seated at a table enjoying a late night snack. They stopped eating and nodded when Hunter and Rowen joined them.

"She's not the one we want," Hunter said as he poured them each a glass of red wine.

"But I will take you to her," Rowen said with conviction.

They listened while Hunter explained. The entire time, Lorena kept her gaze fixed on Rowen's face. When Hunter was finished, he glanced at Lorena.

"She's telling the truth, mon cher. We can trust her," she said with a nod.

Rowen smiled.

"Vampires are living lie detectors," Hunter explained. "It's impossible to deceive them."

"I can also sense that your heart is broken and your grief is real. You two truly loved each other and passionately," Lorena said. "How tragic for you it ended like this."

"I want my mother to suffer as she has made me and everyone else suffer. I want to watch her die so I can spit on her corpse," Rowen said flatly.

"What will become of you afterward?" asked Rick.

Rowen shrugged.

"That does not matter," she said.

Mel was studying her carefully. He knew she wasn't human. He also sensed that she wasn't any sort of demonic entity. Whatever she was, he knew she was relatively harmless. For now, she was a bitter, lonely and deeply sad young woman who wanted to avenge the murder of her husband.

At that point, Montcalm entered the restaurant. He stopped almost in mid-stride when he saw Rowen seated next to Hunter at the table. Hunter motioned for him to join them. Montcalm pulled up a chair and sat down while DuCassal poured him a glass of wine.

Montcalm smiled at Rowen.

"Good evening, Madame. I have not seen you since the funeral," he said as he held up his glass.

She smiled.

Hunter explained it all again. Montcalm nodded.

"I must admit, I am relieved to learn that you are not the one behind our troubles. I am certain that Hunter is also relieved," he said.

"That I am, Colonel," Hunter agreed. "Now, we go after the real monster."

"When do we leave?" asked Rick.

"Tomorrow morning if you like," Rowen offered.

"That's fine with us," Hunter agreed. "We can leave right after breakfast. You'll join us, of course?"

Both Rowen and Montcalm nodded.

"It will be a long journey. Bring enough food for several days—and plenty of ammunition," she said.

Rowen led them far to the north. They rode past the Montmorency Falls and turned due north from there. They went past the Wendake and the First Nations and deep into the woods. The journey lasted five entire days and nights. On the morning of the sixth day, Rowen stopped in the middle of a large clearing. Before them stood a tall, snow-white pine tree surrounded by a circle of two-foot tall stones.

"This is where she lives," Rowen said as she slid from the saddle.

She walked over to the base of the tree and knelt down. They watched as she drew an ancient petro glyph in the snow and uttered what appeared to be a summoning spell. Then she stood and stepped back.

"She comes," Rowen said.

Moments later, a tall, beautiful woman with a sour expression and ice white skin materialized over the symbol. She looked at them, then focused her malevolent gaze on Rowen who was standing with her fists clenched at her sides.

"I've returned, Mother," she said.

"Have you come to plead for forgiveness?" the Cold Woman asked.

"No. We have come to kill you," Rowen replied.

The Cold Woman laughed.

"Think you're up to the task?" she asked Hunter.

"Yes," he asserted.

"You'd better look behind you and reconsider," the Cold Woman said with a smirk.

They turned and watched as several very large wolves emerged from the bushes and bared their fangs. Lorena bared hers at the wolves, as if daring them to attack. A series of howls signaled the arrival of a horde of Apotamkin loping toward the clearing.

"You handle those things. I'll take care of the wolves," Lorena said.

"Are you sure you can handle them?" DuCassal asked as the first wolf bounded toward her.

Lorena seized the animal by the throat, whirled it around and hurtled it at a nearby tree. The wolf struck the tree with enough force to snap the trunk in two. The upper part of the tree then fell between her and the rest of the pack.

She grinned at DuCassal.

"I'm sure," she said.

DuCassal checked his shotgun and ran toward the Apotamkin. The O'Sheas drew their weapons and followed.

"Aim for their heads and don't let them get close enough to bite you anywhere!" DuCassal shouted as he fired two shots, both of which decapitated one of the creatures.

The O'Sheas jumped in with guns blazing and the battle was on.

The Apotamkin snarled and charged, only to be gunned down time and again. They fell quickly in pools of blood only to retreat a few yards, regroup and attack again. Each time, the results were the same and the ground became littered with their bodies and stained pink by their sickly blood as leaked out onto the snow.

One of the wolves got past Lorena and bounded toward Hunter. He whirled quickly and fired his revolver into the wolf's face. The animal's head shattered and it fell dead not three feet from him.

He turned toward the Cold Woman.

He holstered his revolver and took the bow and arrow from the back of his coat. The Cold Woman watched as Hunter fit his arrow to the bow and raised it.

"No arrow can kill me!" she said defiantly.

"This one can!" Hunter said as he drew back the bow.

She sneered and waved her hand. The bow went flying from his grasp and landed several feet away.

She laughed.

It was a mocking, irritating laugh.

Hunter charged and tried to elbow her. To his astonishment, he passed straight through her as if she weren't there. As he did, his entire body became covered by a thin layer of frost and a wave of almost brain-numbing cold surged through him. He landed on the ground behind her, shivering uncontrollably.

"Now you know why I am called the Cold Woman," she said.

Hunter attempted to stand, only to be sent staggering backward by the hardest, most painful slap he'd ever felt. He stumbled back into a nearby tree and slumped to the ground. He rubbed his jaw as the lights came back on.

"Foolish and stupid mortal. You cannot harm me. My daughter brought you here to kill me. Instead, it is you who will die," the Cold Woman said.

While the Cold Woman tormented Hunter, Rowen picked up the arrow, raised it above her head, and charged straight at her. The Cold Woman saw her out of the corner of her eye and turned. But it was too late.

Rowen buried the arrow deep in her heart and twisted it for good measure.

"Die, you monster!" she almost hissed.

The Cold Woman staggered backward and stared in horror at the shaft that now protruded from her chest. Rowen watched as she slowly dropped to her knees and gurgled up vile, luminous ichor. Rowen seized her by the hair, glared at her, and spat in her face. She stepped back and watched as the Cold Woman fell to the ground and emitted a long, sorrowful moan as the life left her wicked body.

As the life faded from the Cold Woman, the Apotamkin slowly faded with her until not a trace of them remained. The wolves also ceased their attack and retreated back into the deep forest.

The long nightmare had ended.

Hunter walked over to Rowen and put his hand on her shoulder. She smiled at him.

"That took courage," he said.

"Not courage, Hunter. Hatred. The people of Quebec can once again live without fearing the night," she said. "So can I."

He turned to retrieve his hat. When he looked back, Rowen was gone. He donned the hat and looked up at the stars.

"Be at peace, Rowen," he said softly.

When they returned to Quebec and gave Marquand and Montcalm the good news, they immediately called for a city-wide celebration. Hunter and the others decided to stay for the festival, which was originally supposed to last only one week.

It lasted two.

When it was over, not a man, woman, child, dog or cat was sober.

Marquand found them at breakfast one morning and insisted they follow him. Curious, they finished their meal and followed him up the street to a small studio on the other side of the Place D'Arms.

"What's going on?" Hunter asked.

"I have brought you here to have your photos taken," Marquand said. "Please be so kind as to humor me."

At Marquand's urging, they entered the room one at a time and posed while a photographer snapped several pictures from different angles. Hunter was the last to endure this. When he came out he walked over to Marquand.

"What are the photos for?" he asked.

"The people have decided to erect a statue in honor of what you have done for us. It will be placed in Place D'Arms. It will depict the five of you standing on top of a mountain," Marquand explained.

"Make that six," Hunter said.

"Six?" asked Marquand.

"Yes. Rowen belongs up there with us. After all, it was she who killed the Cold Woman. In fact, I think she needs to be placed in front," Hunter said. "It's the right thing to do."

Lorena smiled.

Marquand nodded.

"It will be as you wish, Msr. Hunter," he agreed as they shook hands. "Now that the troubles are over and spring is here, I hope you will stay awhile and take in the many pleasures our city has to offer."

Before Hunter could answer, Lorena gripped his arm and smiled.

"Merci, Msr. Marquand. I think we will do just that," she said.

Hunter and DuCassal laughed.

"I know when I've been out gunned," Hunter said. "It's been a while since we've had a vacation and I can't think of a better place to have one."

"Or a honeymoon," Lorena smiled.

Marquand turned to the O'Sheas.

"What about you?" he asked.

"I think we'll stick around for a week or so. There's no need to hurry back to Savannah," Rick said.

"None at all," Mel agreed.

"Excellent. Stay as long as you like. Relax and get to know my city. After a while, you may not wish to leave," Marquand said. "Quebec has such an effect on people at times."

Savannah, two weeks later

Hamilton Birch was very old.

Just how old was anyone's guess. No one really knew. Even he forget the exact date of his birth. To him, time seemed to stand still.

He looked to be in his 60s. Yet he could recall events that happened long before the Second Age and places that no longer existed. He had seen countless friends and enemies come and go and had buried dozens of wives, children and grand children.

Immortality had its benefits.

And its curses.

Here he was, back in Savannah. A city he helped found. A city that had survived the ravages of time intact.

And a place he had not set foot in since 1738.

"My existence has come full circle," he said to himself as he walked up the front steps of the ancient manor on Oglethorpe.

To his surprise, he found the door unlocked. Warily, he opened the door and stepped into the front hall. Then he saw the dark cloaked figure seated on the steps of the grand staircase.

"What are *you* doing here?" Birch asked.

"Is that any way to greet an old friend?" the man asked with a smile.

Birch scowled.

"You are no man's friend," he said. "Especially not mine!"

The man laughed.

"How can you say that after all I've done for you?" he asked in mock indignation.

Birch glared at him.

The man stood and paced.

"You *summoned* me and begged a favor—which I granted—in exchange for something that you have never had any use for. Did I not live up to the bargain?" he asked.

Birch nodded.

"You even signed a contract that specified an exact time period. I have come to warn you that the time has nearly expired—and when it does, you will, too," the man explained.

"So you've come to collect?" asked Birch.

"The terms of the contract are very precise. They must be fulfilled," the man said.

"How much time have I left?" Birch asked.

"Sixty-four days," the man replied. "And not a minute more."

Birch paced the floor. The man watched and smiled. The smile annoyed Birch. That's why he did it.

"That's not enough time," Birch said.

"It will have to be," the man said. "You have no choice in the matter."

Birch watched as he vanished then emitted a string of curses.